ELIZA PROKOPOVITS

Her Accidental Frog

Copyright © 2024 by Eliza Prokopovits

All rights reserved. No part of this publication may be reproduced, stored or transmitted in any form or by any means, electronic, mechanical, photocopying, recording, scanning, or otherwise without written permission from the publisher. It is illegal to copy this book, post it to a website, or distribute it by any other means without permission.

First edition

*This book was professionally typeset on Reedsy.
Find out more at reedsy.com*

Contents

Chapter 1	1
Chapter 2	13
Chapter 3	25
Chapter 4	36
Chapter 5	48
Chapter 6	55
Chapter 7	62
Chapter 8	71
Chapter 9	79
Chapter 10	89
Chapter 11	98
Chapter 12	111
Chapter 13	116
Chapter 14	128
Chapter 15	138
Chapter 16	146
Chapter 17	152
Epilogue	163
Also By Eliza Prokopovits	168
About the Author	169

Chapter 1

Nathaniel Johnson was having inarguably the worst morning of his life.

He'd been expecting a hangover, but this? He'd come to only a half hour ago, and it had taken this whole time to make sense of his predicament. If only he could remember more of what happened last night.

He remembered going out with Wortle to the public house and drinking a shocking amount of ale and blue ruin. Nathaniel made a mental note—reiterating the one he'd made last night—that Wortle might not be the best companion of an evening if he didn't want to end up foxed. After midnight, the memories grew vague, but there had been a bit of an altercation with some fellow in a dark coat. The man had called him out, though Nathaniel couldn't for the life of him remember why. They'd decided to settle their dispute immediately, forgoing seconds. They'd taken a hack to Nathaniel's lodgings for his dueling pistols and then made their drunken way to Hyde Park, which was quiet as death at two in the morning. They'd found an out-of-the-way spot, paced out the distance, and…

And then everything had gone dark. Darker, that is, than the middle of the night in Hyde Park. Nathaniel couldn't remember a thing after that until a half hour ago, when he woke up without an injury, without a headache, without his pistols, and without a clue how he'd ended up in the Serpentine.

As a frog.

It had taken several minutes of splashing and thrashing before he figured it out. But then it couldn't be ignored: the webbed feet, the slick skin, the desperate croaks coming from his own throat. The fact that the reeds along the bank looked so very much taller than he would have expected.

Must have been a bloody magician, he thought grimly. *Dirty cheat. The chosen weapon was pistols, not magic.*

Nathaniel would gladly have settled the score, but he was hardly in a position to do so, besides having no idea of the fellow's name. Served him right for getting into a duel while in his cups. Another mental note: no more blue ruin. Ever.

Then again—no. It didn't serve him right. The man was a cad. Nathaniel wallowed for a few minutes in the unfairness of it all, before shaking himself out of it and looking forward. What was he to do? How was he to break this blasted curse and become human again? Aside from the obvious reasons remaining an amphibian wouldn't do, he had a commitment to attend his father in Devon at the start of June, and too much rode on it to miss. He had two months, but in his helpless state, he was unlikely to solve his problem in two years, let alone a shorter time. His only hope was another magician, but how was he to find one in his current situation?

A voice on the shore froze his froggy blood to ice. "I'll only look for a minute, and then I'll come back." Nathaniel knew that musical voice. His ear had become attuned to it, listening for it at every assembly. It belonged to the person he usually hoped most to see, now the one person he wished to avoid. Lady Hannah Stanton.

CHAPTER 1

***

Lady Hannah Stanton had high hopes for this Season. Not only were her brother Henry and his new wife Kate in town, but her younger sister Mary had prevailed upon their mother to allow her to come out early at just barely seventeen. Hannah was less surprised by this concession than she might have been, though she herself had entered Society at nearly nineteen. Mary was the baby of the family; when she wanted something, she generally got it. With Mama's attention on launching Mary into Society properly, Hannah could enjoy her third Season in London without being subjected to her mother's heavy-handed matchmaking.

Of course, a younger sister's debut also meant hosting a ball for her at the house in Berkeley Square, or at least it did when their parents were the Duke and Duchess of Caulder, even though Mary had already attended half a dozen assemblies and soirees since they arrived in town.

And a ball meant new gowns and fittings and rather a lot of hubbub.

Not that Hannah minded. She loved balls, and she loved Mary and her sister-in-law Kate, who was nineteen, a year younger than Hannah. Kate had grown up extremely sheltered and, until they arrived in town nearly two months ago, had never experienced a true London crush, where the assembly was packed so tightly that one could hardly dance. Mary's experience of balls had been equally limited. Hannah had been looking forward all year to showing her new friend around town while her mother managed Mary's introduction.

This morning, however, had been spent at home in a final fitting for their ballgowns, as Mary's coming-out ball was only three days away. Hannah had stood on a stool in her mother's lavish dressing room while Madame Evangeline, her mother's preferred French modiste, tutted and made a few final adjustments. Sunlight had streamed through the glazed windows, and she'd been so afraid that clouds would take over before she could get outside. At last, they were finished, and Hannah and Mary together rushed out the door, tying on bonnets and tugging on gloves as they went.

Hannah tipped her head back, slowing her stride and letting the sun warm her face.

"That defeats the purpose of wearing a bonnet, you know," Mary teased. "You might as well leave it off."

"If we were at home, I would," Hannah agreed. "But it wouldn't do to shock the *ton* right before your ball."

"But you don't mind if you freckle before the ball?"

Hannah made a face at her sister. They both had the same problem—a little kiss from the sun and their noses and cheeks sported a dusting of freckles. This rarely stopped Hannah from going without a bonnet, but she had high hopes for this ball…. She tipped her head back down so that her face was shaded.

"Now that you've ruined your complexion, could you walk a little faster? I'd like to reach the park before everyone else leaves it."

Hannah picked up her pace. It was a longish walk to Hyde Park, but she loved the wide open green and the curving Serpentine. Mary enjoyed watching the people—on most fine mornings, everyone who was anyone could be seen driving or walking through the park, so that half the time traffic was at a standstill. Hannah preferred the flowers and little glimpse of nature she could get in the middle of London.

Mary needn't have feared. Members of the *beau monde* still

crowded the lanes, greeting each other from horseback or from phaetons or curricles. It would only get busier as the Season progressed and the weather grew pleasanter. The two girls were stopped several times by acquaintances, their pace slowing to a meander. Near the bank of the Serpentine, they fell in with a pair of Mary's particular friends, the Miss Lemmons, Elise and Christine. Hannah allowed her attention to drift as the younger girls chatted excitedly about the prospect of the ball and the other entertainments of the coming week. She noticed several flower beds with tiny green shoots and promised herself to come back in a few days to see their progress. Her gaze settled on the Serpentine, whose still water reflected the rarest of blue skies. Movement near the bank caught her eye, and she took a step toward it without thinking.

"What is it, Hannah?" Mary asked, breaking off from her description of the hothouse flowers Mama had ordered.

"I saw something in the water," Hannah answered, never taking her eyes from where she'd seen the motion. "It might have been a frog, though it's a bit early for them."

Miss Lemmon made a sound of disgust, while Miss Christine let out a little shriek. "*Frogs*? Really?" They edged away from the water, though they were nowhere near the bank where they stood.

"Please leave it, Hannah," Mary pleaded in a whisper. "I don't want to go look at frogs or fish or grasshoppers or… anything that could jump at me."

Hannah bit her lip. When they were children, she used to explore the lake on their estate at Cauldercrest with their older brothers, Henry and Daniel, tagging along regardless of whether the boys wanted her to. Once they'd gone off to school, however, she'd had no one to share her discoveries with, and she'd dragged Mary along on more than one occasion.

"You stay and talk with your friends," she said. "Just keep within sight. I'll only look for a minute, and then I'll come back."

Mary let out a long-suffering sigh but returned to her conversation. Hannah grinned and crossed to the reedy bank. She shot one more glance back at her sister, who was arm in arm with Miss Lemmon and walking slowly. It suddenly struck her as funny how people could be so alike and so different simultaneously. Mary shared the same brown hair, hazel eyes, and sun-induced freckles as Hannah, though Hannah's face was rounder. Mary was only an inch or so taller than Hannah, but she shared the same propensity toward curves rather than the straight, willowy figures of the Lemmon sisters. Both of them loved dancing and music, and both had determination in spades.

And yet, Hannah was certain that Mary would fit into Society much better than she did. Mary was so bubbly and energetic, a natural flirt and gossip, which would endear her to half the *ton*. Hannah had never once been called reserved, but compared to her sister, she felt it. And then there was her inconvenient interest in wildlife…

She turned her attention back to the water and crouched down, holding still and breathing softly as her brothers had showed her so that she wouldn't disturb whatever creatures were there.

***

Nathaniel looked to the bank and saw Hannah crouching down. Her bonnet hid her eyes, but he could see her pretty pink mouth curved in a small smile as she went still and silent. He'd always found that amazing about her, how she overflowed with life one moment and then tamped it all down to become part of the scenery the next. He swam closer, unable to help himself. The movement caught her eye, and he froze under her gaze.

Breathe, he told himself. *She doesn't know who you are. She doesn't know that you've proven yourself to be the biggest fool in London.*

They stared at each other for another moment before she glanced over her shoulder at a cluster of young ladies. Mary must be waiting for her. Hannah sat back on her heels. As she made a move to go, Nathaniel panicked. However he felt about Hannah, he couldn't let this chance pass him by.

"Help," he croaked, swimming closer. "Help."

She froze, staring. "That's not the sound they usually make," she muttered to herself.

Nathaniel hopped onto the bank, stopping several feet from her and holding her gaze. "Help. Please."

"Good heavens," she breathed. "Who are you?"

He'd much rather not admit that.

"Human," he croaked.

She blinked. "Oh dear. *Which* human? What's your name?"

Nathaniel cringed, but there was nothing for it. Confessing his stupidity to the most wonderful girl in England was a fair penance for his foolhardiness last night—and another reminder never to drink, if this was the humiliation that followed. But when he opened his mouth, nothing happened. He couldn't croak a single sound, let alone a word. His name lodged like a rock in his throat. What was happening? He gulped, blinked, and tried again.

Still nothing.

"Do you not remember? Or can you not say?"

Nathaniel was trying, but his name, his father's title, anything that would reveal his identity to Hannah—it was all locked inside him with no way out. He finally tried to say something different. "Help," he repeated weakly.

He sounded pathetic, but at least he got the word out.

"Of course I'll help," Hannah said, reaching slowly toward him and resting her open, gloved hands on the ground for him to hop into. "I'll take you to Kate. She's a magician, and she's got a spell that can pause or undo other spells—I'm not sure how it works exactly, but I've seen her use it." Her hands were warm under Nathaniel's feet, and the kid leather was soft. She slowly raised him up to eye level. "We'll get you sorted right away. Do you mind riding in my pocket for now? Mary's a bit squeamish about things that jump."

She shifted him over to one hand and with the other held open the pocket of her skirt. Then she lowered him slowly into it, and he hopped from her hand and settled against the fabric. The walking dress was dark green and blocked out the light. When Hannah rose to her feet, the swooping motion of her skirt made Nathaniel momentarily dizzy. Coupled with the heady scent of her lightly floral perfume, he felt almost as untethered as he'd been last night under the gin's influence.

A light pressure as she gently put her hand against the outside of the pocket. "Are you all right in there?"

"Good," he croaked.

They both fell silent, which was a relief. Frogs weren't designed for talking, so forcing out a syllable or two with each croak was hard work. He wouldn't have minded listening to Hannah talk, but when she joined her sister and they'd said goodbye to their friends, Mary was the one whose chatter filled

CHAPTER 1

the air. Nathaniel let his mind wander. Mary's conversation had always been filled with parties and gossip, though when he'd first been introduced to the Stantons of Cauldercrest, her parties had been imaginary fêtes held by her dolls. The rhythm of Hannah's walk was slow and soothing, and it lulled him into a state of calm he hadn't thought within his reach.

He could feel when Hannah climbed the steps to the front door and the change in the air when they crossed the threshold. A pause and a rustle, as bonnets and gloves were removed, then a few more steps before Hannah hesitated.

"Have you seen Kate?" she asked.

Nathaniel could hear her mother's voice, muffled slightly by the pocket. "Henry took her to a museum once her fitting was over. I'm not sure which one. Something wrong, dear?"

"No, not at all. Just something I wanted to ask her." The lightness in her voice sounded forced, but only slightly.

More movement, more stairs, and then the closing of a door. A quiet splashing sound that made Nathaniel's skin ache with thirst. Was that possible? Apparently for a frog. Hannah's bare hand slipped into the pocket. Her skin was distractingly soft as she scooped him up and lifted him out. Daylight from the window made him blink a few times before he realized that she was lowering him gently into a washbasin filled halfway with water from the nearby pitcher. It wasn't as cold as the Serpentine, but it was cool and deliciously wet. He splashed and cavorted and delighted in the feeling before settling with his eyes just above the surface. Hannah was laughing, and Nathaniel found he didn't mind that she was laughing at him, because the sound made his heart dance.

"Feel better?" She grinned. She sat on the edge of the bed, and Nathaniel suddenly realized that he was in her bedchamber.

His heart pounded even faster at that. He'd never once seen the inside of this room, nor had he ever intended to. But Hannah was talking again, so he dragged his thoughts back. "We'll have to talk to Kate after dinner. In the meantime, you can stay here rather than suffering in my pocket. Here." She grabbed a small decorative pillow from the bed, the linen cover embroidered with lilies. She set it on the washstand beside the bowl. "Something comfortable if you want to be out of the water. Please stay on this table where you're safe, Mr. Frog."

A groan came out as a strangled croak.

"I know," she said, her brow furrowing. "It's a terrible name, isn't it? But I must have something to call you. You truly can't tell me your real name?"

Nathaniel tried to say his name again, but it lodged in his throat like before. All he could do was blink at her.

"Very well, then, I'll have to come up with something." She studied him. "You're a common frog, *Rana temporaria*, so... I'll call you... Tempo?"

He'd forgotten her impressive memory for scientific names. Hearing her say the Latin name now took him back to the very first time he'd stayed at Cauldercrest when he was fourteen. His father, the Earl of Bembry, had taken his mother on the Grand Tour of Europe. His mother had been lifelong friends with the Duchess of Caulder, and as he and Henry were the same age, he'd been invited to stay with them for the summer rather than being stuck alone at home with his tutor. That summer, in addition to being the start of his lifelong friendship with Henry, was one of the best of his life, full of racing around the estate with Henry and his brother Daniel, climbing trees, riding horses, playing cricket. They'd spent hours searching for tadpoles and minnows in the shallows of the lake. Hannah had left Mary to her dolls and followed the boys around as often as she could. He could still picture her, nine years old, barefoot with her skirt tucked up into the waistband, up to her knees in the water, and telling anyone who'd listen about the types of frogs they might find and what their proper Latin names were. Her brothers had rolled their eyes and humored her, muttering to him that she'd stumbled across some natural history texts in the library and wouldn't shut up about it now.

Hannah raised an eyebrow at him, and he realized she was waiting for a response. "Will that do?"

"Naturalist." It took two croaks to get the word out.

She smiled. "A very amateur one, I suppose. I've always found creatures and plants fascinating." She tilted her head to the side. "So Tempo will do?"

Nathaniel nodded. It was better than Mr. Frog.

"Good. And let's pray that your condition really is *temporaria*." She smiled at the wordplay. "Now, Kate will probably need to know how you ended up this way. Can you tell me what happened?"

If Nathaniel's green skin could have flushed, it would have been beet red. "Duel," he muttered. "Magician." If he could have turned redder, he would have. If there were anywhere to hide in the basin, he would have done that, too. But he had to admit the truth. "Trifle. Foxed."

Hannah's mouth fell open. "You got into a drunken duel with a magician? Good heavens."

He blinked, chagrin and mortification practically oozing from him. "He used. Magic. Not. Pistol."

Her eyes widened. "That's not sporting. Do you know what spell he used?"

Nathaniel shook his head.

"Hmm. Well, hopefully this is enough for Kate to go on. I have to dress for dinner now, but I'll be back to collect you."

She disappeared through the doorway into the dressing room, and Nathaniel sank below the water with a sigh. He hadn't wrestled with such a confusing mix of emotions in years, if ever. Hannah alone raised feelings of elation, humiliation, dread, and joy, and that wasn't touching on the hope and fear that gripped him as he thought of Henry's wife's spells or his helpless fury at the unknown magician. A frog was far too small to contain so much. He swam restless laps in the basin in a vain attempt to control it all.

Chapter 2

At dinner, Kate leaned over to Hannah and said, "Alice mentioned you were looking for me?"

Henry and Kate had been married for more than eight months, and it was still odd for Hannah to hear Kate refer to Mama by her first name. It only made sense for her to do so—Kate was family now, so there was no need for calling Mama "Your Grace," and Kate already had two mothers of her own, biological and adopted. But Kate was one of only three people who used Mama's Christian name.

"I was thinking," Hannah said, aware that Mary was listening, "that we should bring our watercolors to Hyde Park. It was lovely today."

"Oh, yes, let's." Kate's smile was filled with honest delight.

Hannah smiled back and leaned a little closer, lowering her voice. "I also have another dilemma to discuss later."

Kate nodded subtly, and they both returned to their meal.

Later, when the ladies left the table, Hannah looped her arm through Kate's to keep her from following Mama and Mary into the parlor. "Library," she murmured. "I'll meet you there."

She released her friend and dashed upstairs to get the poor frog-man she'd named Tempo. He was just climbing out of the basin onto the pillow when she entered the room. She picked up the towel from the washstand and held it on her open hands. Tempo obliged by jumping on, and she tucked the towel around him. "You'll need to stay quiet and hidden until we reach the library," she told him. "Hopefully, this will all be over soon."

Clutching her little bundle carefully, Hannah hurried down the stairs and slipped into the library, pushing the door closed behind her. Kate, sitting in one of the upholstered chairs, looked up. Her golden curls, which never stayed neatly pinned, glowed in the firelight, and her cornflower blue eyes sparkled with curiosity. Hannah set the bundle down on the table, and Kate moved over to join her. Hannah flipped back the corners of the towel to reveal the frog. His olive green skin with darker brownish blotches gleamed in the firelight. Kate gasped and pulled back.

"Hannah," Kate said slowly, "why do you have a frog?"

"He's the dilemma I mentioned," she explained. "He's really a human, but he got into a duel with a magician while they were both in their cups. I thought maybe you'd have a spell to reverse it?" She held her breath.

Kate turned a mystified gaze from Hannah to Tempo and back. "Who—who do you think it is?"

"I don't think he can tell me. I'm calling him Tempo for now—he's a *Rana temporaria*, you know."

"Is he?" she said weakly.

"Kate," Tempo croaked.

Kate let out a little squeak of alarm. Hannah gasped and put a hand on Kate's arm. "I've entirely forgotten my manners! I should have introduced you. Kate, this is the man—frog—currently known as Tempo. Tempo, this is my sister-in-law, Mrs. Catherine Stanton."

CHAPTER 2

"Call me Kate," the poor girl managed.

"And I'm Lady Hannah Stanton," Hannah continued. "But you can call me Hannah."

"-Ann-" Tempo croaked twice, then shook his head. "Can't say." The *h* sound seemed to be a problem. He turned his protruding eyes on Hannah. "Lady?"

She shrugged. "Why not?" She turned to Kate. "So, what do you think? Will the spell you used to get out of the garden work on him?"

Kate lowered herself into a chair. "I really thought you were testing my gullibility," she said. "But you weren't." She looked at Hannah for verification.

"No, I'm quite serious. I know nothing about magic, and I can't leave him to muddle through as a frog."

Kate looked at the frog. "How can you tell it's a *him*?"

"He's only about three inches," Hannah said. "Females are usually bigger."

Her sister-in-law nodded and studied Tempo some more. "I suppose we could try Harborough's spell. It won't hurt anything…."

"Try," Tempo croaked. "Please." He took a small hop closer to Kate.

She held out her right hand, palm up, and spoke a spell-word that sounded like a nonsense mashup of foreign languages, only a bit of which Hannah recognized. Nothing happened. Kate frowned, closed her eyes, and tried again. Still nothing.

Kate looked up at Hannah. "I'm sorry. It doesn't always work, particularly if I don't know much about the original spell. I'll look through my spell books tomorrow and see if there's anything." A pained look crossed her face, and Hannah knew she was regretting the loss of all the magic books that had disappeared from her tower when her adopted mother vanished without a trace. "Not that *any* of them would have had a counter spell for this," she added in a low murmur.

Just then, the library door opened, and Henry peered in. "Kate, are you in here?" He took in the two of them and their sober expressions and stepped inside, closing the door. "What's wrong?" Then he saw the frog on the table. He sighed. "Hannah, I thought you were past bringing creatures home. You'd better not let Mother see it inside the house."

"It's not like that, Henry," Kate said quietly.

"He's a spelled human," Hannah explained. "I found him in Hyde Park today, and he asked for help. What else was I supposed to do?"

Henry gaped from one to the other. "You're serious?"

"Of course I am. Henry, this is Tempo, for now, anyway, until we find out who he really is. Tempo," a startled look flashed across Henry's face as she turned to the frog to continue the introduction, "this is my brother, Lord Henry Stanton."

"Stanton," Tempo croaked.

"Well, then." Henry ran a hand over his face. "I'll do what I can to help, but I still say you ought to keep this from Mother."

"I will," Hannah said, rushing to give her brother a hug. "Thank you. And thank you, Kate." She hugged her too. Then she gathered Tempo up in his towel and, with a brief goodnight, hurried from the library to return him to his water bowl.

***

Hannah gently placed Nathaniel on the pillow by the basin of water, allowing him to hop in by himself. She hung the towel to dry, talking all the while.

CHAPTER 2

"I'm so sorry, Tempo. I really thought that would work. Kate's spells almost always do. But as I told Kate, I don't know anything about magic, although it does seem as though you need to be rather specific about things, doesn't it? You need to know exactly what you intend to accomplish with the spell, and you need to have the exact right word. It seems awfully complicated."

She disappeared into the dressing room for a few minutes. Nathaniel splashed about in the basin, trying to fend off the crushing disappointment that pressed in on him, along with burgeoning worry.

His trip to the Bembry estate in Devon two months from now loomed just a bit more alarmingly after the failure of Kate's spell. He'd been able to temporarily forget about it during the brief few hours that he'd held onto hope that he could be human by nightfall. Now, however.... It would be different if his father were a kinder, more understanding man, if he were even a decent human being. Nathaniel could somehow have Hannah get word to his father that he was... incapacitated... and unavailable. But his father would never accept an excuse. If Nathaniel didn't come for his annual, fortnight-long visit to discuss the estate and holdings, Lord Bembry would cut off his monthly allowance. Nathaniel had skipped the visit once in a rebellious fit just after leaving university—he didn't like or respect his father, and his father couldn't care less for him, so he hadn't seen why he ought to spend time with the man—and his allowance had been withheld for six long, uncomfortable, penny-pinching months. He had no desire to go through that again.

Not that he needed deep pockets as a frog, but he was rather desperate to be human again eventually.

He splashed in the basin, his only clear conclusion that he couldn't let Hannah know how he was feeling. She was doing so much for him, and it wasn't her fault the spell hadn't worked.

When she returned to the room, Nathaniel was entirely distracted from his thoughts. She'd changed for bed, wearing a dressing gown over her nightdress. Her dark hair had been unpinned and brushed, and it hung long and straight down her back. Nathaniel gaped. He'd never seen her with her hair down, not since they were children and it escaped the ribbon she'd used to tie it. Hannah seemed oblivious to the intimacy of the moment, bustling over to check on him.

"Do you have everything you need?" she asked. "I'm sorry there aren't any bugs for you to eat here, but I'll take you to hunt tomorrow."

Nathaniel nodded, unable to force a single word out. Hannah smiled, her face lighting up in a way that always made his stomach flip, but this time there was sympathy in it too.

Nathaniel closed his eyes as she crossed to the bed and removed her dressing gown. He didn't open them again until he heard the bed creak and she murmured, "Good night, Tempo."

"Night," he croaked.

He sank beneath the water. He'd thought that the disappointment would crush him, but being here with Hannah had tempered it. He was still helpless and angry, worried, and desperate to be human, but if being a frog meant more moments with Hannah, maybe this cloud had a silver lining after all.

***

Nathaniel didn't sleep at all that night. He was restless, and he wished the basin were large enough for a proper swim. He didn't dare splash too much, for fear of waking Hannah. By the time she woke up several hours after sunrise, he was ready for a change of any kind.

"How was your night?" she asked as she slipped on her dressing gown.

Nathaniel kept his eyes closed until he heard her footsteps shuffling closer. He opened one eye to peek at her. Her hair tumbled in a messy brown cloud around her shoulders, and she yawned as she leaned over to put her face on a level with his cushion.

"Did I wake you? I'm sorry. I forgot you're nocturnal."

Nocturnal. That would explain why he hadn't been able to sleep. "Didn't. Wake." He could reassure her of that at least.

"Oh, good," she said with a small smile. From here Nathaniel could see the faintest dusting of freckles across her cheeks and nose. She straightened, and he instantly missed her closeness. "Once I'm dressed, I'll take you outside to find your breakfast. Then you can sleep while I have my own." She slipped out of the room before he could say anything. In a few minutes, she returned. Her morning dress was a persimmon color that suited her unexpectedly well, bringing color to her cheeks and previously unnoticed copper highlights to her hair. She'd pinned her hair up for the day, but a few tendrils framed her face. She was simply beautiful, even as she tied an apron around her waist.

"These pockets should be big enough," she said, gently lifting him and settling him into one. "Hide until we reach the garden, if you please."

Nathaniel braced himself against the fabric as she swept from the room and down the stairs. Before long, he could feel the fresh air. He stretched until he could grasp the edge of the pocket and peer out, discovering a smallish garden—huge to a frog—beset by a gray drizzle.

"Where do you think we'll find the best bugs?" Hannah murmured. There was a whoosh as she flipped open an umbrella and stepped onto the stone path. "Let's try over here." She moved toward a heap of composting vegetation, then scooped him up and set him down. "See anything?" she asked.

He did. Without conscious decision, Nathaniel's tongue lashed out and snagged a fly. He swallowed it with a gulp, thoroughly disgusted with himself, but hungry. He snapped up fly after fly, even catching an unsuspecting cricket. The misting rain felt gloriously cool on his skin, but he knew the damp air would be chilly for Hannah, who'd come out without a shawl or any kind of coat. He ate as quickly as he could, then hopped back to her feet.

"Done," he croaked.

"Are you sure? We haven't been out here long."

"Sure," he said. "Good spot. Ate well."

She grinned in what he thought was relief and put him back into her pocket for the trek back inside. Once he was settled on his pillow and she'd removed her apron, she said a soft "sweet dreams" before leaving for the morning.

Nathaniel was comfortably full and tired from his long, harrowing day and night. He drifted to sleep within minutes.

That evening, Hannah told him that Kate hadn't found anything useful in her books yet. "But she says they're all rather ordinary magic books, whatever that means, and this is unconventional magic, so she wouldn't expect to find what she needs in them. Tomorrow she and I are going to the public library to see what we can find." She chatted on, telling him about the morning calls she'd made with her mother and Mary. Her stories were told in bursts, between trips into her dressing room to prepare for bed. Once she paused in the doorway, absently combing her hair. "I'm babbling, aren't I? You probably find this all dreadfully dull. It's unkind of me to subject you to so much mindless talk when you have no escape."

Nathaniel croaked in protest. It was good to have company after a long day alone, even if he'd spent much of it asleep. And he'd always enjoyed listening to Hannah talk, no matter what she was going on about. She had a way of making even the most tedious morning visit sound interesting. "Please. Do talk."

"Really?" She paused with her brush halfway through her hair. "You don't mind?"

He shook his head. "Good."

She smiled, and his heart flipped again. "If you're sure. Mary's more of a chatterbox than I am, but I do always seem to have a lot to say." Her expression turned wry. "But you're a good listener. Thank you."

"Gladly."

***

The next day went much the same, with a brief visit to the garden for his breakfast before he slept in Hannah's room while she went out for the day. She returned that evening with no good news about her visit to the library.

"Their books are the same books of common spells that Kate has, or even more basic," she explained. "Nothing but simple spells or fancy illusions. We'll be busy all day tomorrow helping Mama and Mary, but after that we'll start searching the bookshops on Bond Street." She sighed. "I'm sorry you're stuck like this."

Hannah moved toward the doorway but paused before going through. "I don't know how I didn't think of this before. Are you married? Do you have a wife or fiancée or someone who will be worrying about you? I can get a message to them for you."

"Not. Married," Nathaniel croaked. He considered asking her to send a note to his father to reschedule his visit for later in the summer, but even croaking his father's name was impossible. Nathaniel sighed. "No. Messages." His father wouldn't worry about him anyway. The only family who might was Hannah's.

"Good." Hannah's shoulders relaxed. "It would have been awkward to explain all this." She disappeared into the dressing room to prepare for bed.

***

Hannah seemed rushed when she returned to the room the following afternoon. "Sorry for leaving you alone all day, Tempo. Mama had me helping with decorations in the ballroom for hours." She sank onto the edge of her bed with a sigh, then tilted her head, considering him. "I don't think I've mentioned the ball yet. It's Mary's official coming out do, and Mama's invited *everyone*."

Nathaniel knew all about the ball, having been invited personally before the invitations had even gone out. He'd promised to come, and more than that, he'd asked both girls to save him a place on their dance cards. His heart sank at the idea of either of them sitting out a dance because he stood them up, but before he could decide how to warn Hannah without the words choking him, she was already on her feet and heading for the door.

Bothered, Nathaniel hopped into the basin of water and swam tiny laps. He stayed in the water for nearly an hour and was just climbing up the side to hop onto his pillow when he heard Hannah say, "I've got to go now, Tempo."

He looked up and promptly lost his grip on the side of the bowl, despite his sticky front feet. He fell back into the water with a splash, righting himself and facing her again, his heart pounding. She looked radiant. Her dress was white silk and lace in the latest fashion, her hair curled and pinned with pearls, and more creamy pearls graced her ears and neck. Nathaniel suddenly flashed back to Hannah's coming-out ball two years ago. He'd been glad for the wall he'd been leaning against when he saw her enter the room because otherwise his knees would have given out. He'd been fond of Hannah for years, but now there was no question that his best friend's younger sister had grown up, and done it beautifully.

Tonight she'd go to her sister's ball, and half the *ton* would see her like this. She'd have no trouble filling her dance card. And not a single dance would be with him.

He let out a disgruntled croak.

"Are you all right?" Hannah stepped closer.

"Can't. Dance. With. You."

"I *am* sorry you have to miss out on the fun, but I think Mama would flay me alive if I brought you along."

He wished she'd caught his meaning, his feeble hint that he would be missing the ball. "Saved. Dance." He tried again.

But Hannah was distracted, tugging her gloves on and

fastening another string of pearls around her wrist. "Hmm? Yes, my dance card is already half full and the evening hasn't even begun."

Nathaniel deflated. His hints wouldn't work tonight. "You look. Lovely."

She looked up at him and smiled. "Thank you, Tempo. I'll tell you all about it when I come back."

She left with a soft swish, and Nathaniel sank to the bottom of the basin, weighed down by his heavy heart.

Chapter 3

Hannah surveyed the crowded ballroom. Theirs wasn't the largest ballroom in Mayfair, but somehow the better half of the *beau monde* seemed to have fit inside. Mary's entrance had gone perfectly, leading smoothly into the start of dancing. Now they'd gone through two sets, and the next was about to start. Hannah stood to one side drinking a glass of lemonade before her next partner found her, looking for the one figure she hadn't seen on the dance floor.

Nathaniel Johnson was tall enough that she should be able to see at least the top of his head above the crowd, though she was *not* tall, and her view was impeded by everyone around her. His sandy hair at least should have been visible. Obviously, she wouldn't be able to see his laughing brown eyes from here, but she wished she could. It had been a week since he'd dined with them in Berkeley Square, a week that felt like months. Why did time have to go off kilter when she thought of him?

"Looking for someone, Lady Hannah?" A low voice beside her drew her attention to her next partner.

"Mr. Wilson," she said, curtsying slightly and downing the rest of her lemonade. "Not looking so much as wondering who is here. Everyone, it seems."

Everyone but Johnson.

"It seems so. Yet none is as lovely as you this evening."

Charles Wilson smiled at her and offered his arm to lead her to the dance. He was a solidly built gentleman of medium height, with dark hair, long sideburns, and startling green eyes. She'd met Mr. Wilson at Almack's last Season, and while he was an excellent dancer, his skills as a conversationalist were somewhat lacking. After the initial compliment, he uttered some poor banalities about the weather. She wondered if he'd fare better on a topic of interest to him rather than the perpetual inconsequences proscribed by the *ton*, but she couldn't imagine what topic to try. He'd bored her to near tears several times.

The dance, at least, was a lively one, leaving little freedom for talk and plenty of opportunity for his dancing skills to shine. That was one mark in his favor; Johnson notoriously had two left feet the moment music began playing.

When Mr. Wilson's dances were done, Hannah was handed off to another partner, and then another. Once, between sets, Mary found her.

"Have you seen Mr. Johnson?" her sister asked, scanning the crowd. Mary was the only one of the family who used Johnson's formal address. Hannah called him by his surname like her brothers, thanks to long summer days spent tagging along with the boys, and Mama called him by his Christian name. "I saved a set for him, but Lord Marcell is asking, and I'm wondering if I should accept him instead."

"Do that," Hannah sighed, her stomach knotting. "I haven't seen him. I'll ask Henry as soon as I have a moment."

Her moment came during the last set before going in to supper. Johnson had asked her and Mary both to save him a set, and she'd chosen this one—the one that would mean he would take her in to the dining room and sit beside her. His absence, therefore, ruined her hopes for not only this dance, but the meal as well.

Henry and Kate had found a spot by a window and were talking quietly. Hannah had no qualms about interrupting their private conversation. Her brother and her best friend were the two people she needed most at the moment, and they could talk all they wanted later.

"Where is Johnson?" she hissed. "He promised he'd be here."

Henry exchanged glances with Kate. "I don't know. Haven't seen him. I sent a man to his lodgings earlier, but no one was home."

Kate laid a hand on Henry's arm, and Hannah could see that they were both just as concerned as she was, if less disappointed. Johnson wasn't one to break a promise, especially to the Stantons. He'd been half adopted into the family after his first summer stay, and even more thoroughly a few years later when his mother had died and his father, never particularly involved in his childhood, had distanced himself even further.

"I'll call on him in the morning," Henry said. "I'm sure it was a simple misunderstanding and that he's fine."

His reassuring smile showed that he knew Hannah's disappointment twined with worry until her stomach was so twisted up that she wouldn't eat a bite of supper.

What he didn't know was that Hannah had made herself a promise at the beginning of the Season. Seeing Henry and Kate so happy together had inspired her to take action on the *tendre* she'd held for Johnson all these years. Though she was afraid he still saw her as the pig-tailed girl who climbed trees with her brothers, she was determined to change his mind. She would win him over, and they would have an understanding by the end of the Season... or she would give him up for good and find a love-match elsewhere. Tonight was supposed to be a step toward her goal, dancing and dining together when she knew she looked her very best. But how was she to win him if he wasn't there to be won?

"I beg pardon for interrupting," Mr. Wilson said at her shoulder, "but would you allow me the honor of escorting you to dine, Lady Hannah?"

It took a great deal of effort to respond affirmatively with a smile. A glance at Kate suggested that the smile had come out as more of a grimace, but Hannah couldn't help it. She didn't want to be stuck with dull Mr. Wilson when she'd had her hopes set on Johnson's charming company. She didn't want to be here at all anymore, crowded by so many people when she was worried over the one who was missing.

She suffered through, however. It was what one did. "Good *ton*" meant pasting on a smile and conversing politely and pleasantly, however little one had in common with one's companion.

It was a relief when the ball ended and Hannah gathered with her family to farewell the guests. Mr. Wilson made a gallant bow over her hand, which sent a flare of annoyance through her. Why did the man keep pursuing her? What could he possibly have taken from their strained and wan conversations that could make him want more?

As soon as she could, Hannah escaped to her rooms. She gratefully shed her gown and donned a nightdress and dressing gown, sitting at her vanity while a maidservant unpinned her wilting curls. The steady brushstrokes soothed her somewhat, calming her. But her mind wouldn't rest. What could have happened to Johnson? Why wasn't he there?

The sky was beginning to fade to gray by the time she crossed into the bedroom. A faint splash reminded her of her guest. In the commotion of the night, she'd forgotten all about Tempo.

"Ball?" Tempo croaked.

She knew he was asking how the ball went, but she didn't have the energy or motivation to give him the full account she'd promised. "It went very well, but I'm too tired to talk about it tonight. Tomorrow," she said.

"Something. Wrong?"

How could a frog read her nearly as well as her brother? Was she that incapable of hiding her feelings? But she didn't want to go into it with him right now. Her disappointment was still too raw. She settled for the barest explanation she could, while climbing into bed and blowing out the candle.

"Henry's friend was absent, though he'd promised to come. We're all a bit worried."

***

Henry's friend.

The words shouldn't have cut like they did. They were absolute truth, and yet hearing them from Hannah caused an ache in Nathaniel that wouldn't subside. That was all he was to her. Henry's friend. Just one of the boys she'd played with as a child, a semi-adopted third brother.

He longed to know if she'd saved a dance for him, if she'd been upset that he'd missed it. But Hannah didn't want to talk, a sure sign that she was exhausted. He would let her sleep. He'd find a way to ask in the morning, and hopefully asking the right questions would reveal his identity.

Nathaniel had fallen asleep on his pillow and the sun was climbing high by the time Hannah rose the next day. Her movement woke him, and he opened one eye. She moved slowly, and he could only guess at how tired and stiff her muscles still were after a long evening of dancing. He knew from experience that even one accustomed to the exercise could be weary after such a long night. She came closer to check on him, her dressing gown tied loosely about her waist, her hair hanging in waves over her shoulder.

"I'm sorry, Tempo," she murmured. "I didn't mean to wake you. Will you be all right waiting until this evening to go hunting?"

"Yes," he croaked.

She nodded. "Have a good sleep."

Nathaniel watched until she was out of the room, then let himself drift off again, a sad sort of wistfulness settling over him.

Hannah returned as dusk was falling, and she was wearing her pocketed apron again over her day dress. Nathaniel had been awake for a quarter hour, splashing in the day-old water in the basin while he waited. He hopped out when she entered the room.

"Did you sleep well?" Hannah asked as she went first to the window, opening it and looking out before carrying the basin over and dumping it. She didn't seem to expect an answer because she kept talking as she poured fresh water from the pitcher. "I'm sorry I wasn't able to take you into the garden this morning. You're probably terribly hungry. I always have so much trouble getting going the day after hosting a ball. But of course we must."

She held her pocket open near the edge of the table and let

him hop in. Nathaniel settled himself, letting her voice wash over him. She must be taking the back stairs, because she didn't seem to worry about anyone hearing her.

"I have yet to understand why gentlemen insist on calling the morning after a ball. It's not as if we'd forget them if they waited another day or two until we were well rested."

She sighed as she opened the door to evening birdsong and the distant bustle of horses and carriages on the street. Nathaniel braced himself as she lifted him from her pocket and set him near the scrap heap. His stomach grumbled as his tongue darted of its own accord to snag several flies and a cricket, followed by a small worm from the edge of the pile. As he ate, Hannah kept talking.

"Mr. Elliot and Captain Franklin came to see me, and Lord Marcell came for Mary. He's a nice enough man, but he's one-and-thirty—practically ancient to Mary's tastes. I think Mama expected more callers to come for Mary, but Mary didn't seem to mind." Hannah clasped her hands behind her and looked up at the small apple tree in the corner of the yard. "Henry took Kate to Bond Street for an hour or two, but they didn't have any luck finding the right spell yet. I'm sorry the solution is taking longer than I expected."

"Not. Your fault." Nathaniel snagged another fly. "Nor Kate's." Anxiety over regaining his humanity hovered around him like London smog, but he wouldn't place that on Hannah. He hated the frown that creased her brow. He changed the subject, hoping it would brighten her expression. "Tell me. About. Ball."

"Right," Hannah said, her frown dissipating as he'd hoped. "I've never seen the ballroom so crowded, and everyone said Mary looked exquisite. She's so bright and bubbly, you know, she's always sure to please. She danced every dance, and Lord Kerr took her in to supper."

Before she could launch into a description of who Mary's partners had been, Nathaniel blurted another question, to get to the information he cared about more.

"And you?"

"I danced most of the evening too." Here her expression fell a little, and Nathaniel missed a passing fly because his eyes were fixed on her. "Captain Franklin was my first partner, and I also danced with Lords Marcell and Kerr, and with Mr. Elliot."

Most of the evening? Had she had to sit out the dance she'd saved for him? Hadn't anyone asked her for it? Or had she been concerned enough at his absence that she'd chosen not to dance?

"'Enry's. Friend?"

Hannah pressed her lips together and shook her head. "Henry stopped to see him when he and Kate drove out, but he wasn't there. No direction left, no instructions to the servants about when to expect him back." The frown was back, and she was biting her lower lip, something she did when she was upset or thinking hard. "He promised to come, and he keeps his word—that's one thing I've always loved about him. I don't know what could have happened."

Nathaniel tried to say "frog" or "me," but neither of those words seemed to be allowed in this context. *Blasted magic.* Nor were "spell" or "duel."

He managed to say, "Acci. Dent," and immediately regretted it when Hannah went pale.

"I certainly hope not. Perhaps Henry should send a groom to ride out of town on the main highways to see if anyone has heard of anything untoward." She twisted her hands in her apron.

Nathaniel hadn't meant to make Hannah worry needlessly that he'd been in a riding accident or set upon by highwaymen. "Surely. 'E's. Fine."

Hannah nodded slowly, still frowning. Nathaniel brought the subject back to the ball to distract her.

"Last. Night," he said, catching another fly. "Supper?"

She didn't quite repress a sigh. "Mr. Wilson."

He felt a twinge of jealousy. Wilson had made his interest in Hannah clear last year. Apparently, he hadn't given up.

She shook her head, as if to clear it, and looked down at him. "Have you finished?"

"Yes. Thanks."

She held down her hands, and he hopped into them. Back into her pocket for the ride upstairs, and then the transfer to the pillow. Hannah watched him slip into the basin of water and splash around a little.

"You really don't have much space here," she said. "Would you like to go to the park tomorrow, if the weather is fine? We'll go early before you need to sleep for the day. It would be pleasant to swim farther and stretch your legs, wouldn't it?"

"It would. Thank you."

Hannah went to bed early that night. "Will you wake me at dawn, Tempo, or should I have one of the servants wake me?"

"I will." Nathaniel agreed, though as the night progressed he wished he hadn't. He wanted to let Hannah rest after how tired she'd been the day before, even if it meant he missed his trip to the park. But he'd promised, so when the sun rose, shining weakly through the thick fog, he croaked, "Lady."

Hannah didn't stir. Nathaniel tried again, a little louder. She made a small sound that was half sigh and half moan and turned her face toward him. Her dark lashes shadowed her cheeks, and her mouth curved up just the tiniest bit. He waited, silent, unwilling to call her again. Her sleep was too beautiful to interrupt.

It was only another moment or two before those lovely eyes fluttered open, and Hannah yawned and stretched.

"Did you call me?" she asked him sleepily. "I thought I heard you."

He croaked wordlessly. She didn't seem to notice that his answer hadn't been a true answer. She merely slipped on her dressing gown and shuffled out the door.

She looked more alert when she returned, in a morning dress and pelisse, with her hair pinned up. Nathaniel was given a place in one pocket of her pelisse, and he stretched up to look out of the top of the pocket, clinging to the edge with his webbed front feet, as she pulled on a pair of kid gloves. They took the back stairs down, as they had last evening, to go into the garden and then out the garden gate to the street.

"No. Footman?" he croaked as quietly as he could.

"I see no need for one." Hannah didn't dawdle, but she also didn't rush, and Nathaniel thought she was enjoying the foggy stillness. "It's too early for anyone to be about, particularly on a Sunday."

That was patently untrue. Street sweepers and other servants had likely been up for an hour or more, and the more inebriated gentlemen would be only just returning home. But arguing required too many words, so he got to the point.

"I can't. Protect. You."

"I wouldn't expect you to," she said. "I don't need protecting."

Again, Nathaniel wanted to argue, but his grumbling came out as a strangled croak. It was his duty as a man and an honorary Stanton to defend Hannah in the place of her father or brothers. But he was helpless and small, and she was uncooperative. All he could do was pray nothing happened and stick close to her.

Hannah stopped when she reached the banks of the Serpentine, near the same spot where they'd found each other days ago. She set him down and watched him hop back and forth on the grass. With a corner of his mind, Nathaniel felt foolish with her watching him bounce around, but it felt so good to stretch his long, powerful legs. He'd been so limited hopping from pillow to basin, and now he could try some really explosive jumps. He splashed into the water then, and swam back and forth, always keeping Hannah within view. The sun rose higher, and the fog thinned. Nathaniel returned to Hannah, hopping around her in a circle to shake off some of the excess water before getting back into her pocket.

"Feel better?" she asked, a trace of a laugh in her voice.

"Much," he admitted. "Thanks."

"I'll try to bring you back more often." She turned and began the walk home. "We can rearrange the furniture in my room so you can stretch your legs in there, too. I just want you to be careful any time I'm not in the room, because the house cats have been known to find their way in sometimes, and I'd hate to think what they'd do to you."

Nathaniel shuddered, and her hand came to rest gently, reassuringly against his pocket.

Chapter 4

The Sunday Hannah took Tempo to Hyde Park before church was the only fine day of the whole week. Rain fell, drenching or drizzling, for the next six days. Hannah carried an umbrella with her each time she took Tempo into the back garden. He ate quickly and hurried them back inside, which struck her as odd, since frogs prefer being wet. Was he being gentlemanly and trying to limit her time in the rain? Thinking of a frog as a gentleman felt silly, but this whole scenario was absurd. Why *wouldn't* Tempo be thoughtful even in the small things?

On Monday morning, Hannah hurried down to breakfast, hoping to catch Kate and leave for Hatchard's before Mama claimed her time or any callers arrived. Kate, however, didn't come down, and Mama insisted that Hannah and Mary accompany her on a call to Lady York, who had an eligible nephew. They were putting on bonnets, pelisses, and gloves in the front hall when Kate emerged, looking a bit pale and drawn.

Hannah hurried over to her while her mother and sister headed out the door. "Are you all right? I was hoping to start our bookshop search at Hatchard's this morning."

Pink appeared in the middle of Kate's pale cheeks. "I… I had some trouble getting started this morning. Henry suggested breakfast in bed." She rested a hand on Hannah's arm. "Don't worry about Hatchard's. I'll have Henry take me later on when I'm ready to go out."

"Are you sure?" Hannah frowned at her sister-in-law. "Perhaps you ought to go back to bed. We can try again tomorrow morning."

"I'm sure I'll be fine," Kate assured her. "I… er… didn't sleep well."

Kate was as bad a liar as Henry, but Hannah let it go for now because Mama wouldn't be happy about waiting. The conversation kept playing through her mind as the carriage rolled through town, however. Why would Kate lie?

That evening, Kate excused herself early to retire for bed. She gave Hannah a significant look, and Hannah followed her into the corridor. Kate turned to her. "Henry and I spent an hour at Hatchard's this afternoon, but no luck. Their selection of spell books is impressive, so it may take a few days, but I'm optimistic."

"Shall we leave immediately after breakfast tomorrow?"

"Let's see how I sleep tonight." A blush bloomed up Kate's neck and ears.

"What is going on?" Hannah hissed. "What are you hiding?"

"Nothing." Kate turned and started walking toward the stairs. "Don't worry about it."

Kate missed breakfast again the next morning, and by the time she left the room she and Henry shared, the first callers of the morning had arrived. Hannah was stuck in the drawing room with Mama, Mary, Mr. Wilson, and the Miss Lemmons. Lord Kerr arrived just after Mr. Wilson left. When all of their guests had gone, Hannah learned from a footman that Henry and Kate had left for Bond Street a half hour before.

This pattern continued all week, with Kate missing breakfast with the family, only to act as if nothing was amiss when she returned from her bookshop search in the afternoon. Hannah was mystified. She and Kate had fallen promptly into a close friendship when they'd met, and she'd thought they kept no secrets from each other. By the end of the week, Hannah had decided that if Kate wouldn't talk to her, Henry would have to. She began to look for opportunities to catch him on his own to demand answers.

Meanwhile, Tempo was also a cause for concern. Each evening, Hannah gave him whatever update she'd been able to wrest from Kate about the search for the spell. She also told him about the other events of the day in as intricate detail as she could, knowing that it must be hard to be stuck in her room being nocturnal while the world of humans went on without him.

Tempo listened raptly to every story Hannah told, but day by day she could see him sinking into a gloomy listlessness bordering on despair. He ate without enthusiasm. Though she had moved the table with the washbasin a few feet along the wall and positioned several chairs in key locations, he used the new course of obstacles for jumping less and less. Whenever she entered her room, she'd find him either submerged and motionless in the basin of water or perched in the center of the embroidered pillow. He perked up slightly when he saw her, but Hannah could sense his low spirits.

"I don't know what to do about him," Hannah groaned to Henry when she finally cornered him in the library the following Monday before dinner. "He's so quiet and mopey, and I just feel awful."

CHAPTER 4

"Why don't you ask him?" Henry suggested. "He's probably bored, but maybe there's something wrong with his water or food? We're doing our best to turn him back—we've gone through all the spell books at Hatchard's and have started on the other bookshops."

"Speaking of which," Hannah rounded on her brother, "what is going on with Kate? I was going to go with her every day this week, but she hasn't been at breakfast, and Mama keeps filling my day before I can talk to her."

"She hasn't been feeling up for company in the morning," Henry said vaguely. "You know she's not used to being around people—even family—all the time."

"But it hasn't seemed to bother her at all in the weeks since we came to town. Why now?"

Henry shrugged.

Despite his being five years her senior, Hannah could read her brother like a book. He was hiding something and doing his best to evade without lying. She opened her mouth to press for answers.

Henry spoke first. "I still haven't heard anything from Johnson. Wortle hasn't seen him in over a week, and he hasn't been at the club either. I'm about to write to his father to see if he's in Devon. I know he goes every year, but usually it's not until June or July."

The abrupt subject change startled Hannah, but her concern for Johnson overrode her determination to uncover Kate's secret. "Yes, do write," she exclaimed. "Is there anyone else he might have gone to see?"

Henry shook his head. "I haven't been able to think of anyone. He has no other family, and most of his university friends are in town for the Season."

"Well, hopefully his father knows something. When are you writing?"

"Now, if you'll leave me in peace," Henry said, giving her a teasing smile and moving to sit at the writing desk. He took out a sheet of hot pressed paper and a bottle of ink. "Go find out what's wrong with your frog. I promise to tell you as soon as I hear anything."

Hannah left him there, forcing herself not to stomp her feet on the way up the stairs to her room. Henry had successfully distracted her from her quest for information. He knew her too well. But now, not only was she curious about Kate and concerned about Tempo, she was also even more worried about Johnson, particularly after Tempo's suggestion that he might have been hurt somehow.

She watched Tempo closely that night, as he hopped from table to bed to floor to chair. He seemed to be bright-eyed and healthy. Had she been imagining his distress?

When he'd splashed through the basin and settled on the pillow, he looked across the room at her. "Trouble. Lady?"

"No," she sighed. "Just a lot on my mind. Something's up with Kate, and Henry's friend Johnson is still missing. And…" Tempo seemed to puff up a little, working his mouth silently, but Hannah pressed on, needing to solve the one problem that was within her purview. "Are you unhappy, Tempo? Do you need more water? Should we go out to catch bugs more often?"

"No. Lady," he croaked. "Need. Nothing."

Hannah wished she could read the frog's expression as easily as she could read Henry's. "Are you sure?"

"Quite."

She accepted his word, as she had other matters on her mind. But when his depressed spirits were still evident two days later, she perched on the edge of her bed so that she could look him in the eye where he sat on his pillow.

"What can I do, Tempo? How can I make this easier to bear? You said you didn't need anything, and you seem physically healthy, but you can't pretend that you're happy. Kate has gone through the entire selection of spell books at Hatchard's, and Henry's been making inquiries of Prinny's Council of Magicians. We *are* trying to turn you back."

"I know," Tempo croaked. "Not un-. Grateful." He hopped from the pillow to a chair and then across to land on the bed beside her. He looked up at her with his bulging eyes. "Just… Bored."

Hannah studied her tiny companion. She could only imagine how bored she'd be if she were stuck in her room all day with only one other person for occasional company. But then… why must he stay in the room? He could fit into a pocket easily enough. As long as he was well-behaved….

"Would you like to attend Lady York's ball tomorrow?" she asked, a smile pulling at her lips as her plans took shape. "I'd take you to Almack's tonight, but I don't quite dare. Can you imagine Countess Lieven if she saw an uninvited amphibious guest? I'd lose my voucher for certain."

"How. Would I. Go?"

"I'll add a pocket to my ballgown. As long as you stay quiet and still, no one will know you're there." She shrugged. "The inside of a pocket isn't particularly exciting either, but it has to be better than seeing these four walls all day and night."

"You'd. Do that?"

"Of course."

"Thanks."

"Would you like to come with me now?" It was just after

breakfast, when Tempo usually fell asleep. "I'm going to get Mary's help to add the pocket to my dress—she's a metaphorical magician with fashion—so it won't be all that interesting, but I don't mind wearing my apron."

"I'll sleep," he said, blinking at her. "But the. Offer. Is ap-. Preci-. Ated."

Hannah smiled sympathetically. Poor Tempo still tried to speak like a gentleman sometimes, but he couldn't hide how difficult it was to croak everything out. She gently lifted him up and placed him back on his cushion.

"I'll come spend a while with you before we leave for Almack's," she promised.

***

Mary was in the music room practicing the pianoforte when Hannah found her. She'd long found her sister's devotion to her music lessons impressive; Mary could be easily distractible with nearly every other subject but music. The two of them had played duets often, with Kate joining them on the harp. Hannah waited patiently by the door while her sister finished the song.

"Is that for your musicale with the Miss Lemmons?" she asked as Mary closed the music folio.

Mary nodded. "Christine is going to sing with me. I'm to sing with Elise on a French number she's working on. Tomorrow they're coming here to practice." She rose from the stool and crossed the room. "Did you need something? Or do you just want to see your most beloved sister?"

"I always want to see you, Mary," Hannah laughed, "but I'll admit, I do have another motive. I need your help with a slight alteration to my dress for tomorrow night."

"For Lady York's ball?"

"Exactly. I want to add a pocket to the dress but in a way that won't be noticeable."

Mary's eyes narrowed. "Is this so you can carry your pet frog with you?"

Hannah gaped at her. "How do you know about him?"

"Hannah, *please*. I'm not a simpleton. And my room is right next to yours. You're always talking to *some*body, and I know what a croaking frog sounds like." Mary plunked her hands on her hips. "Why can't you have a normal pet, like a cat or a small dog? A canary? Why must you always bring home the most awful creatures?"

Hannah blushed and dropped her gaze. She'd brought home any number of small companions growing up, from frogs and newts to caterpillars and mice. It had been years since the last one—Fuzzy Whiskers, the mouse, had been reluctantly released outdoors when she was fifteen—but she'd yet to live down the reputation.

"I found him in Hyde Park," she said. "His name is Tempo, and he needs my help."

Mary rolled her eyes. "You're impossible." She heaved an exaggerated sigh. "But I love you."

"So you'll help me with the dress?"

"As long as you promise—cross your heart—that your frog will not jump on me or near me, ever."

"He won't, don't worry."

Mary continued to look skeptical, but she led the way back to her dressing room, where she had a special chest just for fabrics and fripperies. Hannah hurried back to her own room to pull her ballgown from her wardrobe, carrying it carefully to Mary's room to find her sister with an assortment of silk and lace spread on the floor around her. Hannah draped the gown over the back of a chair, and together they studied it. It was the palest green silk with white lace at the neck and short sleeves. Hannah had elbow-length gloves to match.

Mary circled the chair slowly, then picked up a swath of white silk. She draped it this way and that across the bodice of the dress, humming and murmuring to herself as she did.

While she worked, Hannah asked, "Are you enjoying the start of your Season as much as you expected?"

"Oh, yes," Mary said absently, her attention still on the fabric. "All the balls are delightful, and Lieutenant Carter has already promised to take me driving in the park once the weather clears." She was quiet for a moment, rearranging the silk a few inches, then she added softly, "It would be nice if Lucas Templeton were here, though."

Hannah smirked. Lucas was Kate's younger brother. Mary had formed an instant *tendre* for him when they'd met last May. "It would be nice," she echoed, "but a young man must attend university sometime."

"He's the heir," Mary pointed out. He wouldn't need to work for a living; he'd have the estate and the income it provided.

"That doesn't mean he should neglect his education."

Mary sighed. "No." She reached for the pincushion. "Hold this."

Hannah made herself useful holding the pincushion and the loose silk while Mary attached it to the shoulder and waist of the gown. As Mary's creation took shape, Hannah had yet more cause to be impressed with her younger sister. The new sash was draped and ruched in just such a way that if Hannah added a small pocket to the inside, the folds of gathered fabric would hide it, even if that pocket contained a frog the size of her palm.

The two girls pinned, cut, and sewed for most of the morning, pausing only for an hour to join Mama in the drawing room to receive callers. Mary and Lieutenant Carter chatted away happily while Hannah made polite conversation with Mr. Elliot. He was the second son of an earl, and he worked in the legal profession, though when he elaborated on what he did, Hannah's mind drifted. He was on the wrong side of thirty, with a dusty sounding voice and a receding hairline. He was universally deemed a good sort of man, but Hannah found little to interest her. Instead, her mind circled on how best to sneak Tempo to the ball with her. She didn't know how long he could go without a swim—hours, possibly, but she didn't want to risk him drying out. Perhaps she could carry a flask of water to douse him halfway through the evening? Her concealed pocket was unlikely to hold *that* much. Perhaps she could convince Henry to carry the flask for her in one of his pockets.

After their guests had left, Hannah and Mary got back to work, and by the time they were called downstairs to dine early before dressing for Almack's, the sash was complete. Hannah took some scraps of cotton and flannel back to her room along with the dress so that she could sew the actual pocket and attach it—cotton seemed a better choice to carry a damp frog than silk. She only hoped that making it double thick would prevent any wet spots from showing through.

Hannah ate and dressed quickly, then spent a half hour with Tempo before going to Almack's with her family. The assembly room was crowded with the select members of the *beau monde*. While not considered a diamond of the first water, Hannah didn't want for partners. But unlike at her sister's ball, and despite Johnson's continued absence, she was unable to forget the little frog waiting alone in her room.

Upon returning home, Hannah sat on a chair in her bedroom and unpinned her hair while talking to Tempo.

"You didn't miss out on much," she told him. "Almack's was hot, crowded, and reeked of sweat and perfume. And the lemonade was warm and weak." She sighed and began combing her hair. Her small companion followed the brush's movement with his bulbous eyes. "It's all about being seen and making connections with other elite of the *ton*, not about enjoying yourself. I much prefer private balls, and even more, I prefer country balls. There's more space to dance and fresher air to breathe."

Tempo tore his gaze from her hair and blinked at her face. "You don't. Like town?"

"I do," she said. "I like how there's always something to do or someplace to go, and there are friends I only see when I'm here. But solitude is rare, and genuine, levelheaded people are even rarer."

Tempo gave an odd little hiccuping croak that Hannah thought might be a laugh. It was the first one she'd heard from him, and she couldn't help smiling.

"Do you like town?"

"Other. Than. Magicians. And. Duels? Yes."

She could only describe the frog's expression as rueful, which was such an odd look that it made her laugh.

"But I. Like the. Country. Best," he went on. Hannah was surprised by how much he was talking. He usually kept his answers short. "Sunshine. Lakes. Riding. Hunting." He blinked up at her, and she felt like maybe there was a significance to his look, like she was supposed to read between the lines of what he was saying, but she hadn't a clue what more he meant. He opened his mouth as if to speak again, then closed it with a snap.

"Well, we'll keep doing our best to turn you human again in plenty of time to spend the summer in the country," Hannah assured him. "And starting tomorrow, I'll try to give you your share of amusement here in town."

She braided her hair loosely down her back and crossed into the dressing room to change for bed.

Chapter 5

Nathaniel couldn't deny that his spirits had risen drastically following Hannah's offer to take him along to Lady York's. Not that he much cared about attending a ball where he wouldn't be dancing or socializing, but it was a change to the boring routine and his endless anxious thoughts. It was time spent with Hannah. Her kindness toward a pathetic amphibian only made him admire her more.

Hannah spent what felt like forever getting ready in the dressing room, and Nathaniel swam in the water basin the whole time. If he was going to spend the next several hours holding still in a dry pocket, he wanted to get as much water and exercise before they left.

Hannah entered the room, carefully adjusting her sash as she did. His heart leapt. Each time he saw her, he thought she couldn't look any more beautiful, but then the next day she surpassed herself. The light green of her dress brought out the green in her hazel eyes. The sleeves were short and puffed and left half her shoulders bare, giving a clear view of the graceful curve of her neck. A string of pearls rested on her collarbone. Pearl pins held her elegantly curled hair. When Hannah was satisfied with the drape of the sash, she raised a hand to the

CHAPTER 5

two silk rosettes pinned to the right of her curls.

"Mary made these for me," she said, "to make the sash look more intentional. Are you ready?"

Nathaniel was speechless, so he hopped out onto the towel that rested on the table. He dried off as best he could, then held perfectly still as Hannah's soft hand picked him up and tucked him into a pocket sewn cleverly behind the sash.

"Are you comfortable enough?"

He could hear Hannah's voice through her ribs as well as through the fabric. Nathaniel squirmed around until he'd found a position he could rest in for hours, snuggled against Hannah's warmth.

"Good," he croaked.

He could feel her adjusting the ruched silk again and imagined her studying her reflection in the mirror to see if a bulge showed.

"Mary's a genius," she said. "No one will notice if you stay still and quiet."

"I will," he agreed. "Promise." He wouldn't do anything to jeopardize this or any future excursions in Hannah's pocket.

Hannah went downstairs to join her family in the drawing room as they waited for the carriage to be ready. Lady Alice and Kate both complimented Hannah on her dress. She immediately gave credit to Mary, turning slightly to show them the rosettes Mary had made.

"I'll have to let Mary at one of my gowns," Kate said.

The duchess added, "She has a good eye. The line of that sash is very flattering on you, dear."

Nathaniel silently agreed, and he regretted for the briefest moment that his position was behind that sash and not out where he could look at her.

The carriage was announced, and the six—technically, seven—of them all crowded in. A light, steady rain fell. When they arrived at Lord and Lady York's house a few minutes later, footmen with umbrellas took turns escorting the ladies into the house. Nathaniel didn't dare lift his head to glimpse the room, but Lady York had hosted a ball in their opulent drawing room last year, and he remembered that it was a small affair. He could guess by the murmur of voices that there would only be eight or twelve couples dancing at a time, just the type of small, private ball that Hannah confessed last night that she preferred.

Nathaniel listened as Hannah greeted acquaintances. Several gentlemen petitioned her for dances—the only voice Nathaniel recognized was Wortle's—and she accepted. He felt a flare of jealousy each time, but Hannah's responses, always pleasant and amiable but showing no particular attachment or regard, set him at ease.

She greeted a Miss Clarke, who immediately complimented her dress. "Who is your modiste?"

"Madame Evangeline," Hannah said, "but my sister has a gift for turning even the simplest gown or bonnet into something extraordinary. The sash and rosettes were her doing."

"Well, you look lovely. And if I know the ladies in this room, you'll soon see sashes becoming a trend."

The two girls chuckled before separating.

"I feel a fraud," Hannah murmured so softly she could only be talking to him. "If they knew *why* Mary had added the sash…"

Nathaniel gently patted the fabric that separated him from her, since he couldn't croak a response. He didn't want her to judge herself by what other ladies of the *ton* thought. She was an original, and he loved her that way.

CHAPTER 5

The dancing began. Nathaniel was grateful that the pocket was tucked up close against Hannah's torso and not among her swishing skirts. As it was, the motion took some getting used to and made his head spin. Hannah danced first with Lord Marcell and then with a Lord Tarrock—Nathaniel only vaguely knew him from a hunting party a few years back—followed by Mr. Elliot. Each of them conversed by rote, feeding Hannah the same worn out compliments and remarks about the abysmal weather. Wortle, though Nathaniel would never wish for either Stanton girl to be shackled to him and had lately sworn off drinking with the man, at least had something new to say.

"Heard anything from Johnson lately?" Wortle asked as they moved through the dance.

Hannah's voice sounded high and strained. "Why? Have you?"

"Not a word. I thought Stanton might, Johnson being close with your family and all. I haven't seen him in weeks. Never there when I call."

"Oh." Her disappointment was audible. "No, Henry hasn't had word of him. I believe he wrote to Lord Bembry to see if he'd been called home urgently."

It would have to be something urgent indeed to drag Nathaniel away from town to attend his father in the country. The Earl of Bembry had rarely had time to spare from his claret and mistresses for his son or his wife, and now Nathaniel only deigned to spare time for *him* because he controlled Nathaniel's purse strings. The thought of a letter apprising his father of his disappearance made his stomach sour. He could only imagine what Bembry's response would be. He wondered if frogs could vomit because he felt like he might.

To his relief, the song ended moments later, and after

thanking her partner, Hannah wended her way through the crowd. Cool air reached him through the layers of fabric. What was going on? To his surprise, Hannah's silk-gloved hand slipped into the pocket and pulled him out. She stood by an open window with her back to the room. She set him on the window ledge and leaned against the casing. Nathaniel hopped carefully along the ledge, which extended several inches past the window frame, to where the light drizzle dampened the stone. He settled there, looking past Hannah at the room beyond. Lady York's drawing room was as he remembered: yellow floral wallpaper interspersed with several extravagant mirrors that reflected back the candlelight and made the room appear larger.

Hannah, half turned away from the gathering, was partially in shadow, but Nathaniel could see her well enough to tell that something was troubling her. Was it worry over him? Did it bother her so much that her brother's best friend had gone missing? A twinge of guilt twisted in his gut. He'd never imagined that his poor choices would cause the Stantons such anxiety. He'd need to try harder to tell Hannah the truth of who he was. He'd tried hinting several times, but she'd missed them all. If only the magic weren't so very strict about his words and intent. He would try a more roundabout method, somehow, but this wasn't the time or place. He wasn't supposed to be here, and he'd promised to stay silent and still.

They stayed by the window for only a few minutes, enough for Nathaniel's skin to get wet and for Hannah to regain her composure. Before long, he was back in the pocket, and Hannah was dancing again with no one the wiser.

Once at home, Hannah pulled Henry and Kate aside. It was well past midnight, but Nathaniel could feel Hannah's tension

CHAPTER 5

and restlessness even through the pocket.

"Have you heard *anything* yet?" she pleaded. "Lord Wortle was asking about Johnson, and if he hasn't had word either…"

"It's too soon yet to hear from Bembry," Henry said. Nathaniel thought his friend was trying to sound soothing, but he could hear the worry in his voice. "He's surely only just now receiving the letter I sent. I've spoken to everyone at the club who knows Johnson, and no one has seen him in weeks. I even stopped by Gentleman Jackson's salon, but Johnson's missed his last three lessons—he's never missed one before."

A sense of foreboding settled over the room. Nathaniel needed to tell them. His friends were suffering. But from his place in the sash pocket, he couldn't tell if they were alone, and he didn't dare talk without knowing. He tried patting Hannah through the fabric of her dress, hoping she'd somehow connect the idea of the man they were discussing and the frog she was carrying.

"You'll be the first to know when Henry hears anything." Kate's voice was warm and calm. "Won't she, Henry? You'll tell Hannah before you even tell me."

"I will," Henry agreed.

"And perhaps tomorrow would be a good day to take our watercolors to the park," Kate continued. "We haven't painted since we came to town, and art soothes the soul."

Hannah sighed. "It does. I'd like that. After a late breakfast?"

Kate must have nodded because Nathaniel didn't hear anything else. Hannah began walking again, mumbling to herself that no amount of painting could ease her soul right now. Nathaniel's heart ached to have caused her pain.

Closed in her room, Hannah set Nathaniel on the pillow beside the water basin. Before he could say a word, she disappeared to the dressing room to change. When she returned, her eyes were shadowed, and she looked both emotionally and physically exhausted.

"Lady," Nathaniel said, already working to find the right words.

But Hannah, rather than sitting to have a chat, flopped onto the bed and threw the covers over herself as if she had no energy for anything more. "I'm done in, Tempo," she said. "We'll talk in the morning. But you did enjoy yourself, didn't you?"

"Very. Much."

"Good. Goodnight, Tempo."

"Night." Nathaniel sighed. Tomorrow he'd tell her. Somehow.

Chapter 6

The next morning dawned fair. Hannah slumped down to the breakfast room later than usual, not surprising after what time they returned home from last night's ball. Kate wasn't at the table, nor did she appear before Hannah had finished eating. Frowning, Hannah knocked on the door of the dressing room Kate shared with Henry.

Her brother answered, still in his dressing gown and looking rumpled. "Kate's not up yet," he said with a huge yawn. "She's not feeling quite herself this morning. Give her an hour or two."

Hannah scowled at Henry. Something was up, but she knew she wouldn't get a straight answer out of him. She stalked off to her own room to gather Tempo and a book to occupy her while she waited.

An hour later, clouds rolled in, and a thick, misty veil obscured the window. "We shan't be painting today," she sighed to Tempo. "I suppose it's better to be prevented from going at all than to go and be caught in the rain." But that didn't stop her from being disappointed.

Kate didn't join her downstairs for another hour, and when she did, she looked tired and drawn. "I'm not used to the late nights and crowded balls," she said, sinking into a chair. "This

Season is taking more out of me than I expected."

She met Hannah's gaze but quickly looked away. Hannah was sure that while what Kate had said was true, it wasn't the full truth. But they settled amicably to embroidering, and Mary joined them, spreading trimmings across a table in one corner before taking an old bonnet to pieces in order to remake it in the latest style.

Tempo snoozed beside Hannah on the arm of her chair, waking up occasionally and hopping onto her lap to get a closer look at what she'd sewn. Mary startled whenever he moved, but she merely teased Hannah for her taste in pets and avoided coming near her sister's seat. When Mary had finished remaking her bonnet, she offered to add a sash to another of Hannah's ball gowns.

Hannah accepted gratefully. "I don't know if you're simply bored and in need of a project or if your love for me truly outweighs your distaste for Tempo, but thank you. I mean it."

Mary laughed. "You don't let me at your wardrobe often enough," she said, gathering the bonnet and some of her materials to return to her room. "I could make you the most admired lady in the *beau monde* if you'd let me."

"I'm sure you could," Hannah grinned. "You're amazing. But I have enough suitors as it is, so I'll settle for pockets for my frog."

Mary rolled her eyes as she left the room.

Mama joined them a little later. Hannah surreptitiously scooped the sleeping Tempo into her apron pocket, and Mary and Kate both kept mum.

Tempo stayed with her all that day. Hannah liked having him nearby, and she thought he seemed happier too. When she took him to her room for a water break, he splashed as energetically in the basin as he had when she'd first brought him home. He really must have been simply lonely and bored.

That night, as they had no engagements, Hannah went to bed early with a book. Tempo hopped to the pillow beside her to read over her shoulder. Hannah barely made it through one paragraph before her eyelids drooped and the book sagged to one side.

"Lady," Tempo croaked.

Hannah jerked awake just enough to close the book and blow out her candle before falling asleep for real with her amphibious companion by her side.

Kate was absent from breakfast again the next morning. Hannah had stopped expecting her. Henry came down just long enough to tell everyone that Kate was feeling under the weather, so the two of them would be staying home from church. Hannah and Mary exchanged concerned glances, but their brother escaped before they could demand answers.

None of Hannah's dresses for church had a pocket for Tempo, so he slept in her reticule until they returned home. She changed into a morning dress and apron, settling the sleepy frog into a pocket before going downstairs.

Mama and Mary were sewing in the drawing room, and Hannah had just settled herself when Kate came in.

"Are you feeling better, dear?" Mama asked. "Henry said you were under the weather, and you *do* look a bit pale. Should you go back upstairs to rest?"

"I'm fine for now," Kate said, twisting her hands together. "There's actually something I need to tell you. It's not fit to discuss, but you're family, so…" She drew in a deep breath, and Hannah held hers. "I'm expecting!"

Hannah's mouth fell open as Mama sobbed and Mary

squealed. Kate was pregnant? That was the big secret? Not that Hannah had been in company with any expectant mothers, but she now recalled something about stomach illness being common, especially in the mornings.

"I'm such a hen-witted ninny!" she whispered, half to herself, half to Tempo, who'd probably woken up in the hubbub. The signs had been right there, but she hadn't put them together.

She stood and hugged Kate as Mama said, "No wonder you've been ill! Are there specific things that trigger your illness? When I had Daniel, I couldn't even look at a baked apple without it turning my stomach."

"Eggs," Kate admitted, sinking down onto the settee beside Mama. "Regardless of how they're cooked, I can't be in the room with them." She gave Hannah a wry smile. "That's why I've been taking breakfast upstairs."

"Oh, how awful," Mary said, her eyes wide in morbid fascination. "What else?"

"Sometimes the texture of potatoes," Kate said, blushing. "And certain types of soup."

"Well, that's easy enough to rectify," Mama said, standing. "Let's go speak with Mrs. Prescott and Monsieur." She helped Kate to her feet and guided her from the room in search of the housekeeper and chef. "And, don't forget, dear, I've carried four children of my own. You're welcome to come to me with questions, however shocking they may seem. If you can't speak openly with family, what hope do you have?"

Mary and Hannah stared after them as the door swung shut. Then Mary burst to her feet. "I have to go tell Elise and Christine. Such news!" She dashed from the room. Hannah chuckled, knowing that a carriage, footman, and abigail would be promptly pressed into urgent service for the call on the Miss

CHAPTER 6

Lemmons.

She gently extracted Tempo from her pocket. As expected, he was awake and blinking sleepily at her.

"Question. Answered," he croaked.

Hannah smiled. "Yes, I finally have the answer to the mystery. Though I could have figured it out on my own if I hadn't been so—"

"Not 'en-. Witted." Tempo gave her a glare.

She opened her mouth to argue, but changed her mind. "Very well. Propriety dictates that such an 'interesting condition' ought not to be discussed around young ladies, so I've only heard the vaguest rumors of what it entails. I could hardly be expected to recognize the symptoms."

Tempo gave one firm nod. The gesture was so entirely unfroglike that Hannah laughed.

"You'll be. Aunt," he said.

Hannah's smile broadened. "It will be great fun to have a child toddling around. I have pleasant memories of when Mary was small—she's four years younger than I am, you know, and she was the sweetest little thing. I used to carry her around with me like a doll. Not that I intend to do any such thing with my niece or nephew."

She stood and crossed to the window, where weak sunlight was trying to brighten the dreary day. "I'm very happy for Kate," she murmured. "She has always wanted a big family. She has three younger brothers, but she didn't meet them until just last year. And you should hear her go on about how she longs to have cousins." She grinned. "She'll be a wonderful mother."

"What. About. You?" Tempo asked from his seat on her palm. "Do you. Want. Children?"

"Yes. Seeing Henry and Kate—I want every bit of what

they have. But I'll have to fall in love first." That was a bit much to confide in a frog, and yet it wasn't entirely true. She'd already fallen in love with Johnson. The trouble was convincing him to return the sentiment. Which seemed more and more impossible the longer he was absent. "Do you?"

"Same."

"How many children?" Hannah asked. "I know it's all in God's hands, but if you could choose."

"'Ouseful." He watched her intently. "You?"

"A houseful?" Hannah thought about that. "I suppose it depends on the size of the house. Cauldercrest is enormous, and I'm not sure I'd want to single-handedly fill it. Perhaps a smaller house. I do love having a big family, and I love it when our cousins all come at Christmas and the house really is full."

Memories of holidays with family visiting washed over her. Two of her older cousins had children, and chaos and hijinks were a constant. Hannah loved it. She remembered the first Christmas after Henry had gone to university, when he'd brought Johnson home with him for the holiday. His friend had fit into the family as if he'd always belonged, playing with the children, joking with the parents. Kate had experienced her first Cauldercrest holiday last year, and she was at least as excited as the youngest children.

"I love. That. Too." Tempo's croak pulled her back to the present. "Happiest. Memories." His bulging eyes were fixed on her. "I want. That."

Hannah was a little surprised. She hadn't realized that Tempo had a large family, though she supposed she didn't know much of his past, or really anything about him. But he had told her there was no one to write to about his condition.

"You'll have it," she said. "Or at least you'll have a fair shot.

CHAPTER 6

We'll find the spell and turn you back, I promise." Hannah raised her hand with Tempo so that she could meet his eyes as she gave her word. "I know I've been saying so for weeks now, but we won't give up until you're human."

"I know." Tempo's gaze was serious. "I trust. You. Lady."

Chapter 7

The gown Hannah chose for Lady Sterling's ball was a coppery red-gold that brought out the highlights in her hair and the color in her cheeks. The sash Mary had added was a deep blue, and she'd fashioned a small headdress to match.

Tempo, as was becoming his habit, complimented her when she entered the bedchamber, though it took several croaks to manage the word "exquisite."

"Always the gentleman," she laughed, scooping him up and lifting him so their eyes were level. "Thank you, Tempo, darling."

With him settled in his pocket, she skipped downstairs, feeling unusually light.

Lady Sterling's ball was another private affair, though larger than Lady York's. Hannah, arm in arm with Mary, followed after Kate, Henry, and Mama, who'd been friends with Lady Sterling for years. In fact, it seemed her mother knew *everyone* in town. Hannah was acquainted with many of them, now that she was in the middle of her third Season. They stopped to greet many acquaintances on their way into the ballroom, including Lady Rampion, Kate's birth mother. Lady Rampion shared the same golden curls and cornflower blue eyes as

CHAPTER 7

Kate. They could pass for sisters if it weren't for the fine lines beginning to form at her ladyship's temples and around her mouth.

"I didn't know you were in town!" Kate exclaimed.

"I hadn't planned on coming this Season, but I found myself with too much time on my hands in the country," Lady Rampion said, brushing a light kiss on each of Kate's cheeks. "I joined Lord Rampion yesterday."

Kate and Henry stayed to chat with Kate's parents, while Hannah and Mary continued to make the rounds with Mama. Lord Kerr was the first to approach Hannah for a dance, which she accepted willingly. Just as the set ended, another gentleman appeared at her elbow. He was handsome, with fine-boned features and hair that curled charmingly around his ears. His blue eyes sparkled flirtatiously.

"Forgive me for accosting you without a proper introduction," he said with an elegant bow, "but I'm impatient and couldn't wait to meet the loveliest lady in the room. Lord Trellion, at your service."

Hannah blinked in surprise, but smiled involuntarily. "Lady Hannah Stanton."

"Are you engaged for the next set, Lady Hannah Stanton?"

"I am not."

"Will you do me the honor?" He gave another flourishing bow and winked at her.

"If you insist." Hannah was pleased to hear how cool her voice sounded, giving no sign of the fluttering that had erupted in her stomach.

Don't be a goose, she told herself as he led her to their place in the set. She was nearly one-and-twenty, too old to get nervous flutters from a common flirt.

But the disobedient flutters refused to abate. Lord Trellion had a way of teasing and flirting that felt so smooth and natural, even while saying things that from anyone else would have been commonplace. It gave Hannah the tiniest thrill to be the subject of such attentions. Most gentlemen were on their best behavior with her, trying to make a good impression on the Duke of Caulder's elder daughter, as she was a wealthy heiress with two very loving and protective brothers. Only Johnson ever presumed to flirt with her, and from him it was the lighthearted teasing of an older brother's closest friend. He never *meant* anything by it.

So Hannah allowed herself to be entertained by Trellion's attentions, trying to forget Johnson for a moment and the fact that she'd rather have her toes stepped on in a dance with him than be swept off her feet by anyone else.

Mr. Wilson had the dance after Lord Trellion, and in contrast, he seemed duller than ever. Two other partners succeeded before Hannah needed a break. She found Henry in a discussion with a small group of gentlemen. She caught his eye from a few yards away and nodded toward the balcony door. He gave her a small nod and returned to his conversation.

Hannah, meanwhile, made her way to the balcony, relieved to find it empty. She took a deep breath of the cool air and pressed her hands to the stone railing, then gently extracted Tempo from her pocket. She set him on the railing.

"Henry will be out in a few minutes with water for you," she murmured to the frog. She'd asked her brother to carry a flask since the day had been clear. "He thinks I'm being ridiculous, you know, carrying you around everywhere. But at least he knows you're more than just a simple pet."

Footsteps sounded on the stone behind her. Hannah looked

over her shoulder, expecting to see Henry. Instead, she saw Lord Trellion's lithe figure and seductive smile. She turned to face him, positioning herself to block Tempo from view.

"Lord Trellion," she said, her heart rate rising. The flutters returned, but they were different now. Something about his expression made her uneasy.

"Lady Hannah," he purred, allowing his gaze to drift from her face to her feet and back. "How delightful to find you out here."

"Henry will be out momentarily," she said quickly. "He's bringing me a drink."

"He was a bit tied up when I passed him. Can I help you in the meantime?" There was a flash in his eyes that made his question suggestive of something scandalous, though the words were perfectly innocent.

"No, I thank you." Hannah backed against the railing, suddenly uncomfortable. Her hands gripped the stone. "I am quite well."

"You *look* quite well." His voice was a low, smooth purr, and his gaze slipped downward again.

Hannah wished fervently that she'd dragged Kate outside with her. She didn't want to be alone. Trellion stalked forward, closing the distance like a tiger on its prey. The balcony was small; Hannah had nowhere to go, no way to get past him. She prayed that Henry would come out any second.

Trellion stopped when he was a half step from her, not touching her but closer than was proper. "I am glad for a moment to speak with you alone," he murmured, and she could smell a blend of wine and mint on his breath. "You quite took my breath when I saw you across the room. You look simply ravishing, and I can't help but wonder—"

His words cut off with a startled cry. Hannah gasped at the sight of the frog clinging to the handsome lord's face. She held out her hands to catch Tempo as he fell away, clutching him to her as Lord Trellion spluttered and swore in disgust. When he'd recovered himself slightly, he looked from Hannah's face to the frog in her hands, his face twisting in revulsion.

"How horrid," Hannah managed, unable to decide if she was appalled, horrified, fearful, or amused. "But he's such a sweet little thing, isn't he?"

Lord Trellion turned on his heel and stalked from the balcony, still spitting a foul diatribe unfit for a lady's ears.

Hannah breathed a sigh of relief and slumped back against the stone balustrade. "I'm afraid you might have gotten me into trouble, Tempo," she murmured weakly. "But thank you."

Another gentleman appeared in the doorway. Mr. Wilson stepped forward, concern etched on his features. "Are you all right, Lady Hannah? I heard a commotion."

Hannah forced a smile. "I'm fine, thank you."

Mr. Wilson's gaze dropped to the frog in her hands. "Is that...?"

She loosened her grip, opening her hands so that her palms were cupped together around the little creature who had gone quiet and still again. "I found him in Hyde Park," she explained. "I call him Tempo."

"*Rana temporaria*," Mr. Wilson said, smiling at the frog before meeting her eyes.

Hannah's forced smile became more genuine. "Precisely. You're interested in natural science?"

"Quite." Mr. Wilson beamed. "Are amphibians your favorite, or do you like all creatures?"

"All," Hannah said, "but I've been partial to frogs for some time. I'm also fascinated by botany."

Mr. Wilson's green eyes studied her for a moment. "You're an original, Lady Hannah. I knew, somehow, you were different from other ladies of the *ton*." He hesitated. "May I… call on you tomorrow?"

Hannah was momentarily speechless. The most boring gentleman she knew shared her interest in wildlife. "I, er, I'd like that," she stammered.

Just then, Henry emerged onto the balcony, his eyes somewhat wild. "Hannah, are you all right? What is going on? Trellion just stormed off the balcony cursing like a sailor. Lady Sterling had him shown out."

Hannah shivered. A light tap on her hand drew her attention to Tempo, who was patting her palm lightly, almost soothingly with his front foot. She took a breath and let it out slowly, using one thumb to stroke along the frog's back.

"I'm fine, Henry," she said finally, glad that her voice sounded normal. She met her brother's eyes. "Lord Trellion thought to get a bit… familiar, and Tempo jumped in his face." The humor in the situation struck her harder than it had before, now that her brother was here and the danger had passed. She giggled. The solemn gazes from the two gentlemen facing her sobered her quickly. "Mr. Wilson came out to see what the commotion was."

"If I'd known there was a problem, I would have come sooner," Wilson declared.

"I wish you'd waited for me inside," Henry said quietly. "As it was, I was unpardonably rude to several people just to get out here as soon as I did."

Hannah laughed, and even Henry's expression lightened somewhat. "Henry, you couldn't be unpardonable if you tried."

Mr. Wilson chuckled and shook Henry's hand before excusing himself to go back inside. Henry crossed to the railing as Hannah set Tempo back onto the stone ledge. Her brother pulled a small silver flask from his pocket and opened it, slowly dripping water onto the frog's mottled olive back.

"You're a good man, Tempo," Henry muttered. "Thank you for looking after my sister."

Tempo gave a faint, wordless croak.

Hannah looked up at her brother. "I'm in trouble now."

"You did nothing wrong," Henry said firmly.

"No, I mean Tempo. I brought a frog to a ball. Everyone here will know about it by the end of the evening, if they don't already. Mama doesn't even know about Tempo." Hannah bit her lower lip.

"Don't worry about it." Henry replaced the flask in his pocket and put an arm around her shoulders. "Mama knows how you are with pets, and let's face it—the Caulder name carries some sway. You won't be ostracized. If anything, you'll set a trend and every young woman will have a pocket sized creature to carry around with her."

"Hopefully they won't all be enchanted humans," Hannah said with a rueful smile at Tempo. "I'm benefiting from the situation, but I wouldn't wish such a condition on anyone."

Henry gave her shoulders another quick squeeze before releasing her. "Agreed. The bookshops were a bust, but we're not giving up."

"Thank you, Henry." Hannah stood on tiptoe to kiss her brother's cheek.

She held out her hands for Tempo, who hopped neatly into her cupped palms. He settled into her pocket, and they returned to the ballroom. Henry's assurances hadn't completely alleviated her apprehension, and she held her breath as she rejoined the company. Right now she wanted more than anything for Johnson to be her next partner, a familiar face who always knew just what to say to lighten her mood. Without him around, her heart thundered with nerves. Tempo must be able to hear it, pressed against her abdomen, and she felt a few more light pats against her ribs. She took a deep breath. That was the best part of her new "pet," however unconventional she would look to the rest of the *ton*. She wasn't alone.

They left the ball early, only a few sets later. In the carriage, Mama demanded to know what all the gossip about Hannah's frog was about. Chagrinned, Hannah pulled Tempo from her pocket. Mama gasped, then put her fingers to her temples and shook her head slowly.

"Hannah, dear, must you? Carry it around the house all you like, but to a *ball*?"

Her brows drew together as she looked down at Hannah's dress, at the sash from which she'd revealed the frog. Mama rounded on Mary. "You knew?"

Mary shrugged. "I tried to stop her, but when has she ever listened to me about her ridiculous pets?"

Mother turned to Henry and Kate next. Kate blushed, and Henry echoed Mary's shrug.

"So everyone knew but me?" Mama cried.

"I didn't know," Father said. He patted Mama's knee and took her hand in his, giving Hannah an indulgent smile. "But I can't say I'm surprised. I'm more astonished that she didn't do this when she first came out."

Hannah wanted to point out that a magically entrapped human hadn't asked her for help two Seasons ago, but she thought it best if Tempo's secret were limited to Henry and Kate. "He's very well behaved," she said instead.

Mama pursed her lips but argued no further. Hannah settled back into the seat, letting Tempo ride on her lap, relieved that Mama's reaction had been more exasperation than anger or disgust.

Once in the solitude of her bedroom, Hannah let Tempo splash in the basin while she brushed out her hair.

"Why did you do it?" she asked. Had he been able to sense her discomfort? Had he known Lord Trellion when he was human?

"Rake," croaked Tempo simply. He swam a few more laps before climbing out and settling on the pillow. He fixed Hannah with a beady stare. "Didn't. Like the. Way he. Looked. At you."

Warmth pooled inside Hannah, and she blushed. Why should the concern and protectiveness of a *frog* make her feel so cared for? But it was obvious to her that Tempo was a good man. Henry or Johnson would have done the same thing in his place, she was sure. "I didn't like it either," she admitted. Her brush strokes slowed. "Thank you."

"At your. Service. Lady."

Hannah braided her hair and went to change. A glance in the mirror showed her that she was smiling without even realizing.

Chapter 8

Nathaniel had spent half the night watching Hannah sleep. He repeatedly caught himself staring, studying the softness of her relaxed features, the silkiness of the hair that had escaped her braid and fell across her cheek. Each time, he reminded himself that a gentleman wouldn't spy on a sleeping woman, and he turned away. He may be in a frog's form at the moment, but that was no excuse for poor behavior.

But the events on Lady Sterling's balcony had shaken him as much as they had Hannah. He was acquainted with Trellion. The man was a hardened rake, but he had always targeted merchants' daughters or recent widows. He knew better than to target a woman in Hannah's position, prestigious and protected. So Nathaniel had more or less ignored the cad, their social circles only overlapping an infinitesimal amount. When Trellion had followed Hannah onto the balcony, however, Nathaniel had been instantly on guard. It hadn't been a lie to say that he didn't like the way Trellion looked at her. He hadn't liked the way the man had spoken to her either. A frog may be cold-blooded, but his blood had heated to boiling at the lord's presumption.

He'd slowly cooled down once Trellion was gone and Hannah

was protected by Wilson and her brother. Wilson's request to call on her had led to another spike of irritation, but Nathaniel grudgingly respected him for coming so quickly to check on her.

He couldn't be happy about Hannah spending time with any gentleman, but at least Wilson was a decent fellow.

So he watched her sleep, wishing for all kinds of things that were equally out of reach.

In the morning, Hannah carried him to the back garden to eat then let him ride in the pocket of her apron to breakfast. There was a long pause after her mother wished her a good morning. Then the duchess said, "Is your frog in your pocket? Is that why you've been wearing an apron so often?"

Nathaniel knew without seeing that Hannah was blushing. He stretched himself up on his long back legs so that he could peer out of the pocket. Lady Alice smothered a little startled "oh!" before fixing her daughter with a firm stare.

"Not at breakfast. Honestly, dear."

Hannah sighed and marched back up to her room. "Did you have to poke your head out?" she muttered.

"She'd have. Sent me. Away. No. Matter. What." He'd been at Cauldercrest for enough of Hannah's childhood pets to know how her mother would respond.

Hannah allowed him to hop onto a chair in the bedroom and then untied her apron. "I suppose you're right. She's never allowed me to bring pets to meals. I don't know why I thought the rule would change for you."

Nathaniel settled in to nap while Hannah went back downstairs. Several hours passed before she returned, making enough noise in the dressing room to draw his attention.

"Lady?" he croaked.

"Coming, Tempo," she called.

A minute later, she appeared in the doorway, having changed into a honey-colored walking dress. She was settling her bonnet over her hair.

"Going?"

"Mr. Wilson has come, just like he mentioned." She tied the bonnet's ribbons beneath her chin. "William Jackson Hooker, the botanist from Scotland, is giving a lecture today, and Mr. Wilson thought to take me." She beamed. "Mr. Hooker is becoming quite well known for his study of mosses and ferns. Would you like to come?"

Nathaniel blinked sleepily at her. Botany had never been of particular interest to him, mosses even less so, but her enthusiasm was adorable, and he didn't want to miss it. Nor did he like the idea of Wilson having her adorable enthusiasm all to himself. He croaked an affirmative.

"Excellent." Hannah grinned at him. "I have an idea so that you won't miss anything."

She disappeared to the next room and returned a moment later with a silk scarf draped around her neck. Picking Nathaniel up, she settled him on her shoulder where he could grip the collar of her dress, and tucked the silk lightly over him.

"How's that?" she asked. "You'll be able to see and hear everything."

Nathaniel couldn't care less about seeing and hearing. Hannah's floral perfume invaded his senses. It should have been cloying this close, but instead it was intoxicating. He'd put up with a thousand lectures on the most uninspiring plant life if it meant sitting here.

"Are you comfortable?" she asked when he made no answer. The perch was precarious, but her nearness made him fearless.

"Very," he croaked. "Walk. Slowly."

Hannah laughed. "A lady never hurries," she intoned, repeating some nonsense she'd been taught in the schoolroom. If frogs could snort, he would have. He'd seen Hannah run more times than he could count. "A lady always glides with poise and grace." She demonstrated by sweeping smoothly from the room.

Wilson met her in the entrance hall and offered his arm. Outside, he guided her to his coach and handed her in. Once the carriage rolled off, Wilson said, "I beg you'll forgive me for the suddenness of the invitation. When you mentioned your interest in botany last evening, it reminded me of this lecture, but I wanted to check the time and make sure I could arrange for seats on such short notice before I made promises I couldn't keep."

"I don't mind at all," Hannah assured him. "It's very thoughtful. I rarely have the opportunity to listen to a true scholar on the subject."

They fell to discussing Hooker's studies and published work until the carriage rolled to a stop and Wilson assisted her out. Nathaniel could see through the light silk that they stood outside a small theater, one that he'd never attended himself but that stood near Covent Garden. They entered the darkened foyer and proceeded to find their seats. The theater was nearly full, not difficult because it couldn't have fit two hundred people. Hannah settled herself into her seat, raising her hand as if to rearrange her scarf, but Nathaniel read it as a silent way to check on him. He patted the skin just beside her collar to let her know he was fine.

Before long, the botanist was introduced and took the stage.

CHAPTER 8

Nathaniel was surprised to find the man so young. Only in his early thirties, if he were to guess from his voice and stature. Nathaniel couldn't get a good view through the scarf, but he'd have expected an older, white-haired chap.

Despite the speaker's energy and evident love of the subject, Nathaniel found himself nodding off. He couldn't muster enough interest in ferns to fight the soporific effect of a warm lecture hall. Hannah's perfume and scarf cocooned him. He fought to stay awake, wanting to be able to talk with Hannah later about something that she found fascinating. He resented Wilson's shared interest. But it was a hopeless cause. Nathaniel succumbed, cozying up against the warm, soft skin of Hannah's neck and drifting off.

He jerked awake with a start when cool air and mid-day sunlight assaulted him. Hannah immediately put her hand up.

"Is something wrong?" Wilson's voice came from Hannah's opposite side.

"I... I brought Tempo. I thought he'd appreciate a chance to get out and see something new, but I think he fell asleep."

She lifted the scarf away from Nathaniel, taking him carefully in her hand. He blinked up at her, still disoriented. Wilson's face appeared at her other shoulder, frowning down at him.

"Poor dear," Hannah murmured. "I wasn't thinking. Frogs are nocturnal, and he hasn't had his daytime sleep yet." She tugged on the mouth of her reticule and set Nathaniel inside. Then she pulled the strings so that it closed almost completely, blocking out the worst of the brightness. "There. Get some rest, and we'll have you home in no time."

She began walking, and Nathaniel tried not to think about her arm linked through Wilson's. He tried not to listen to Wilson complimenting her on her care for her pet. He tried to repress the jealousy that burned inside him. He failed on all accounts.

Nathaniel dozed again as the carriage rolled back toward Berkeley Square. When he woke again, he was in Hannah's room, and she was opening the reticule and lifting him onto his pillow by the water basin.

"I'm sorry, Tempo," she said, regret dampening the excitement he could see in her eyes. "I should have thought that you'd be tired. I shouldn't have forced you to come."

"Not forced," Nathaniel croaked. "I chose. To go." He hopped into the water and sank down so only his eyes were above the surface. She couldn't possibly read a frog's expression well enough to know that jealousy had been his driving force all morning, but no harm in hiding.

"I suppose so," she agreed reluctantly. "But I oughtn't to have asked you. I haven't looked out for you nearly as well as you have for me."

"Please." He scrambled out of the basin. No way would he stand for her going off with Wilson without him knowing. "Want you. To ask."

"Even when I know that the outing will put you to sleep? You didn't notice, but I was stifling yawns myself this morning, and I *like* plants. You still want me to invite you along to those?" Her tone bordered on incredulous.

"Yes." Nathaniel hopped to the edge of the pillow. "I like. Being. With you."

She froze in the middle of removing her gloves. Her expression softened, and she tilted her head as she considered him. "And I like having you around," she said finally. She resumed tugging the fingers of her gloves. "I hope we can find the spell for you soon, of course, but I'll miss you when you're human again."

Hannah left him there to sleep, but it took a while for him to doze off again. He'd been clinging desperately to the hope of being human again in time to travel to Devon, but suddenly it seemed like a loss to return to being no more than her brother's best friend. Perhaps it was time to gather his courage and, once he was rid of the curse, change their status quo.

***

Hannah found Henry in the library. "Tempo's asleep." She sank into the wing-backed chair opposite his. "He fell asleep in the middle of the lecture."

"I don't blame him," Henry said, his mouth curving up. "What did you say it was about? Ferns?"

"And moss." Hannah said seriously. Her brother's nonplussed expression was priceless. She pressed her lips together to fight her smile, but failed and started laughing instead. "I know I have the oddest interests."

"Did *you* enjoy it, at least?"

"I admit, it *was* a bit dull. I prefer flowers and trees to mosses and ferns, and I prefer them even more if I can be outdoors looking at them myself. But it was very kind of Mr. Wilson to think of me," she added fairly.

"Indeed." Henry's mouth quirked up a bit more. He knew how lukewarm Hannah's opinion of Mr. Wilson had been until last evening. Changing the subject, he asked, "What brings you to find me this afternoon, then? Are you merely bored because your little friend is asleep? Or do you want to see what books Father has on the subject of mosses?"

"Do you think he has any?" Hannah asked innocently. She

grinned. "Actually, neither of those reasons. Have you heard yet from Lord Bembry?"

"Not today." Henry ran a hand through his hair. "Should be soon, though. I'm running out of people to ask and places to look."

Hannah sighed, though the news wasn't unexpected. "I also wanted to tell you that I saw a sign in Covent Garden—they're performing Vivaldi's *Four Seasons* starting next week. I thought you and I could bring Kate. We talked about it the first time we met, do you remember?" Hannah and Kate had discussed nearly every possible subject at their first meeting, except Hannah's fascination with natural science. She had wanted to make a new friend, not frighten her off. "I believe I even promised to take her one day."

"I believe you did." Her brother smiled. "I'll purchase tickets. Kate will be thrilled."

Hannah grinned and bounced to her feet. "Perfect."

Chapter 9

The next day bloomed into one of those rare, glorious, sunny days that reminded Hannah how dreary the weather in London generally was. After taking Tempo out to the garden for his breakfast, she knocked on Kate and Henry's door.

Henry opened it in his dressing gown, scowling. "It's a bit early to be knocking, Hannah."

"Sorry," she apologized quickly. "But it's a spectacular day, and I thought Kate might want to paint with me in the park later, if she's feeling up to it."

"I'll mention it to her. I'm sure she could do with some fresh air."

Hannah left them to their private breakfast and went downstairs for her own. Mama and Mary had shopping to do, and Hannah was only too willing to decline their invitation. She had enough experience to know that shopping during the Season was one of her least favorite activities. All the streets and shops were crowded, and there were so many people to stop and talk to that they only ever managed to accomplish half of what they set out to do.

"Kate and I are going to draw in the park later," she said. "Henry thinks the fresh air would do her good."

"Quite right," Mama agreed, promptly supporting the plan. "There's nothing like a walk in the fresh air when you're feeling poorly."

Mama and Mary took the carriage after breakfast, and Hannah sewed in the drawing room for another half hour before Kate came down. She looked more like her usual self, with her golden curls escaping her pinned-up braid and her eyes bright.

"Thank you for the suggestion of going to the park," she beamed. "I had been thinking that very thing when I saw the sun this morning. Only let's not paint. Let's bring our sketchbooks and draw so that we can go without all the fuss and bother of servants."

As much as Hannah enjoyed watercolor painting, she couldn't deny that going about town with just Kate was more fun than trailing servants carrying supplies. Not that she'd had much time with Kate alone since they'd been in town. Between Kate's sickness each morning, Henry's desire to show her the sights, and Hannah's responsibilities to Mama and Society, they'd either gone their separate ways or been together in company with the family. Excitement hurried her steps as she skipped upstairs to gather her spencer, reticule, and drawing supplies.

"I'm going to Hyde Park with Kate," she told a drowsy Tempo as she tied on her bonnet. "Would you like to come? I know it's time for you to be sleeping, but it might be nice to swim a bit."

"Yes. Thanks."

With Tempo settled into her reticule, Hannah rejoined Kate downstairs. They were just pulling on their gloves when Vernon, the butler, appeared with a stack of letters on a silver tray.

"The mail was late today," he said.

"Anything for us?" Kate asked.

Hannah stepped up and sifted through the letters. They looked like mostly invitations to card parties and teas, but one caught her eye. "This one's addressed to Henry." She held it up for Kate to see. They exchanged a speaking glance, both sure that this must be the long-anticipated response from Lord Bembry.

"He's in the library with your father," Kate said.

Hannah snatched the letter and raced off, Kate hot on her heels. They burst into the library, cutting Father off mid-word.

"You have a letter, Henry." Hannah waved the folded paper as she stumbled to a stop.

Henry jumped from his seat and took it from her, slicing the seal with his penknife. He unfolded it, his eyes darting across the page. His face fell as he skimmed its contents. "It's from Bembry," he said, confirming their guess, "but he doesn't know where Johnson is any more than we do. Hasn't seen him since last summer." He scowled. "The old codger declares that he won't bail him out of any trouble, and if Johnson doesn't come in June as planned, he'll cut him from the will."

Hannah huffed out a breath but bit back the unkind things she'd like to say about Johnson's father. None of the Stantons held a favorable opinion of the earl, so their disapprobation needn't be spoken.

"Well," Kate said slowly, "at least now we *know* he's not in Devon."

"Now we know," Henry echoed, his glare fading into a worried frown. It was bad enough not knowing what had happened to Johnson. It was much worse to have a deadline for finding him.

Even the brightness of the day didn't lift Hannah's spirits much as she and Kate left the house. They walked the several blocks to the park, settling onto a bench with a sweeping view of the expanse of grass, scattered trees, and the Serpentine, which glinted in the sun. Once released from the reticule, Tempo hopped slowly toward the water.

Hannah watched him go before opening her book to a blank page and readying her charcoal. But her mind was too full to focus on the beautiful view. "Johnson seems to have well and truly disappeared," she said, shaking her head slowly. "But that's *impossible*. Isn't it? One can't simply *vanish*."

Kate shrugged. "I don't profess to know what is or isn't possible. I've heard all kinds of strange tales, but I doubt most of them are true."

Hannah bit her lip to hold back a sigh. Where could Johnson have gone? Why would he have left? And the thought that sank her heart the most: what if he never returned?

It would force her hand, for certain. If he was gone for good, she'd *have* to give him up and try to fall in love with someone else. She'd begun to suspect that Mr. Wilson might not mind filling that position. But Hannah wasn't ready to give up on Johnson yet. They still had a few more weeks.

After a few minutes of silence, Kate said softly, "Do you remember when I asked if you knew how it felt to be in love?"

"Of course." It had been the day Kate had admitted to Hannah that she loved Henry, which had been plain to see for months.

Kate shot her a sidelong glance. "If I were to ask you the same question today, how would you answer?"

Hannah stared at the scene in front of her, quite forgetting that she was supposed to be drawing it. "I've been sweet on Johnson since I was nine years old," she admitted finally. "He came to stay with us for the summer, and I used to tag along with the boys. Daniel repeatedly told me to 'bugger off'—forgive my language, those were *his* words—and Henry grudgingly tolerated me. But Johnson never seemed to mind. He showed me how to catch tadpoles."

Kate smiled. "Is that where your fascination with frogs began?"

Hannah shrugged. "I'd always been interested in wildlife, but yes, that's probably when frogs gained their special place in my heart." She smiled wryly. "He spent a lot of summers with us. His mother passed on a few years later, and we sort of adopted him into the family. I remember the first time he came after her funeral, I felt so sorry for him that I walked right up and hugged him. I told him we'd share our mother with him since he didn't have one anymore. My brothers always squirmed and pulled away when I hugged them at that age. Johnson didn't. He just hugged me back."

"How old were you?" Kate asked.

"Eleven? Twelve?" Hannah turned the charcoal over in her hand, watching it flip end over end. She said wistfully, "I used to hope that he'd notice me when I came out. See me not as the little girl who used to follow them everywhere but as I am now. I imagined him proposing before the end of my first Season."

Kate's smile held a world of sympathy. "But that didn't happen."

Hannah drew a few lines on her blank paper. "It didn't. I truly don't think he sees me as anything but Henry's tagalong sister." She sighed. "I promised myself that this would be the last Season I'd hold out hope for him. If I can't convince him to offer by the time we return to Cauldercrest in May, then it's time to let these feelings go and find someone else."

Kate frowned, and Hannah knew she was aware how problematic Johnson's disappearance made things. But Hannah didn't want to talk about Johnson anymore. Her stomach clenched with sick fear for him. She cast about for another topic.

"Henry mentioned the other night that the bookshops were a bust. Do you have any idea where else to look for the spell for Tempo?"

Kate looked reluctant to change the subject, but she only sketched for a moment, frowning slightly, before saying, "I don't. I think it's time to explicitly ask for help."

"How?"

"Alice and her friends seem to know everything about everyone, correct?"

Hannah made a face. The older ladies of the *beau monde* were the queens of gossip. "They do. But I'm not sure I want them telling everyone that my frog is an ensorcelled human."

"Oh, I'd never tell them that," Kate assured her. "But I think it's common enough knowledge by now that I'm a magician. No one will think twice if I ask for the name of a practicing, university-educated magician to assist me with a spell I'm having trouble with."

"You're brilliant," Hannah said as she outlined a tree. "They're sure to know of several. And the mail today was full of invitations."

Kate's expression brightened. "It was—full of invitations from people who want to see for themselves the unusual lady who takes her pet frog to a ball."

Hannah snorted. "If my scandalous absurdity opens up an opportunity to find the spell for Tempo, I'm content."

This lighter tone continued for the next hour. Kate told Hannah about her trips with Henry to the famous locales within London, and Hannah told Kate about the lecture she'd attended with Mr. Wilson.

"He's interested in natural science as well?" Kate mused. "If only he'd led with that fact. He might have made a better impression."

Hannah giggled. "I did write some cutting things to you about him last year."

Tempo returned, glistening wetly in the sun as he hopped slowly over. Hannah settled him into her reticule, certain that he'd be asleep within minutes.

"All right, I have to ask," Hannah blurted after turning to another blank page in her book. "How do you feel about… your condition?"

Kate grinned. "You're allowed to say the words, especially to me. You're my nearest confidante outside of Henry, after all. I'm *pregnant*," she added in a whisper.

Hannah giggled. She loved Kate's candor and openness. Kate had grown up away from Society, so the rules of what to say and how to act hadn't been ingrained as deeply in her. She often said whatever was on her mind, even if she ought to have dissembled.

"Very well," Hannah said. "How do you feel about this baby you're expecting?"

"Overjoyed," Kate said. "And overwhelmed." She smiled wryly. "I have no idea what I'm getting into, but I'm so excited I can barely contain it."

"You've always wanted a big family."

"And I've gained more siblings in the past year than I ever thought possible," Kate agreed. "This is a new adventure, a whole new generation of family. It's amazing. I feel like I'm part of something bigger for the first time in my life."

Hannah thought about that. Kate had been alone except for her adopted mother for years; now she was a daughter, a sister, a wife, and soon to be a mother. Her children would inherit the Caulder title, extending the illustrious lineage. Kate finally had the connections and belonging that she'd craved.

"I'm also relieved," Kate continued, darting a look at Hannah. "You know my mother struggled to have children and… well, you heard her story. I'm so grateful not to go through that."

Hannah laid a hand on Kate's arm. "I'm glad you don't have to go through it either. But you would have made your own choices, not hers." Lady Rampion's quest for children had led to Kate being raised away from her family.

"Speaking of my mother, I haven't told her yet. I haven't seen her since Lady Sterling's ball." Kate grasped Hannah's hand. "Will you call on her with me today? It would be easier for me if you were there."

Kate's relationship with her newly discovered parents was improving, but it was still awkward.

"Of course I'll come." Hannah squeezed Kate's hand. "Let's go now. I'm not getting much drawing done anyway."

"Neither am I." Kate snapped her book shut. "But I'm glad we came." She stood and smoothed her skirts.

Hannah rose and gathered her things. "So am I." She hadn't realized how much she'd needed the heart to heart with Kate. It wasn't like she had no one to talk to, but Kate was one of the few people who saw and understood her, whom she genuinely connected with.

As they left the park, she remembered a conversation she'd had with Johnson about the subject. It was late in her first

Season, a month or two before Henry had met Kate. Johnson had appeared at the house one morning before calling hours, joining them for breakfast.

"Would you like to go for a ride, Lady Hannah?" he asked after his first bite of bacon. "I'm afraid you haven't been able to ride as often in town as you do in the country. A friend lent me a sweet mare who would carry you well."

Hannah's heart had swelled so much it nearly choked her. She had, in fact, missed riding dreadfully, and his thoughtfulness touched her.

The chestnut mare was a darling creature, and Hannah had delighted in trotting next to Johnson on his bay. Ambling through the crowded park must have seemed abysmally slow to a gentleman of four-and-twenty with such a superior steed, but Johnson cheerfully kept pace with Hannah, who surveyed Hyde Park with fresh eyes. Everything seemed brighter, greener, and friendlier from horseback.

"How are you enjoying your first Season?" he'd asked.

"It's quite entertaining," she'd said.

"And?"

"And what?"

"I know you, Hannah. That was the truth, but not the whole truth."

Hannah had blushed under his inquiring gaze. "It *is* entertaining," she insisted. "But I guess I thought…"

He waited patiently for her to continue.

"I don't know what I expected. I knew there would be new acquaintances, and I've met *scores* of people, but I guess I hoped I might make a few friends."

"Have you not? You just said you've made acquaintances."

"But acquaintances and friends are entirely different things.

They're all pleasant to be around, but a real friend is someone who understands you, someone you can't wait to tell about the exciting thing that just happened, someone you can bare your soul to. Mary has friends like that at Cauldercrest—Miss Lewis and Miss Helen Winton are just her age, and they're inseparable when they're all in the country."

"And you don't have that?"

Hannah had shrugged. "Mary is too young; Henry and Daniel are too old. Besides, Henry has you, and I'm not sure brothers count, anyway."

Johnson had chuckled. Hannah had always loved his laugh, but now that he was older and his voice had deepened, the sound sent a thrill down her spine. She'd blushed again and looked away bashfully.

"You think I'm spouting nonsense," she'd said. "I always talk too much. I'm ruining a perfectly lovely ride."

"Not at all. I like listening to you. Your perspective is refreshing."

Hannah had hesitated, then ventured, "Do *you* have a friend like that?"

"Gentlemen aren't known for 'baring their souls.'" He'd grinned and raised an eyebrow. "But I'd say I have one or two." He'd looked like he might say more, but he'd clicked to his horse as they came to an open stretch and they'd broken into a short canter.

Thinking back on the conversation, Hannah realized that she had, in fact, been "baring her soul" to Johnson. She'd thought he was only Henry's friend, but he'd been hers too. Kate had become the confidante she'd wanted so badly, but Johnson had been there all along. She missed him.

Chapter 10

Nathaniel spent the entire time in Hyde Park wrestling with the shock and anger that came along with hearing of his father's letter. He'd already been half asleep in Hannah's reticule, but he'd woken fully due to the violent jostling as the girls ran to Henry with the letter. His head felt wobbly after that unpleasant ride, and Henry's words only made the sensation worse, stunning him completely. Nathaniel hadn't expected kindness or generosity from Lord Bembry; he'd long since given up on hoping for basic decency from the man. His father's unwillingness to bail him out of a potential scrape was no surprise.

But to be cut from the will! He'd predicted that missing this year's visit—or even postponing it—would result in his allowance being withheld. Such measures had worked to ensure his compliance last time. And the fear of it had been enough to amplify his anxiety as each week passed with no further hope of reversing the curse.

Now his father—the blasted cad—had increased the stakes to a ruthless degree. A few lean months, Nathaniel could have managed. No hope of an income or title or land? That was a bigger problem.

A much bigger problem, as Nathaniel was increasingly

determined to marry Hannah once he regained his true form. He might have to work to make her see him as more than Henry's friend, but the past weeks had convinced him that he needed her in his life daily.

If his father cut him out… he could take on a profession. He could find employment and earn a modest income. But that wasn't the life he wanted to give Hannah. And worse, if she were to mistakenly believe that he was offering for her hand merely because he needed her money…

His only hope was to pray that Kate found a spell before it was too late.

***

Hannah hadn't wanted to accept Miss Chamberlain's invitation to tea, but Mama had insisted. Her mother was one of Mama's friends and a genteel if air-headed woman. The daughter, by contrast, was a sneering, entitled harpy. Hannah forced herself to count her meager blessings as the carriage rolled toward Grosvenor Square. Kate and Mary had come with her. Tempo was in her pocket. Miss Chamberlain was incapable of entertaining herself, so there were sure to be a half dozen other young ladies present. Try as she might, Hannah couldn't come up with anything to add to the list.

The three Stantons were shown into the drawing room where, as predicted, eight young ladies sat chatting. The drawing room had been done up in peach, coral, and gold, opulent and warm but rather overdone. The ladies, who ranged in age from legitimately fearing spinsterhood, like Lady Charlotte Antoine in her sixth Season, to fresh from the schoolroom like Mary, all rose and greeted them with handshakes and curtsies and a few cheek kisses. They all took their seats again. Hannah and Mary took a small loveseat, with Kate in the chair on Mary's other side and Hannah beside Lady Charlotte. Miss Chamberlain poured tea, and plates of pastries were passed around. Hannah could feel several pairs of eyes on her, though when she looked at any particular lady, gazes were hastily averted.

Once everyone had been served, Miss Chamberlain regarded Hannah coolly. "I heard the most astonishing rumor about you the other day, Lady Hannah. Something about a spectacle at Lady Sterling's ball."

Mary snorted, an entirely unladylike sound. "It was hardly a spectacle."

Hannah nudged her with her elbow. Mary quickly raised her teacup and took a sip.

"I can't imagine what you might have heard," Hannah said, holding her teacup and saucer on her lap and making no move to eat or drink.

"Is it true you have a pet frog?" Lady Charlotte blurted. "And you carry it in your pocket?" Her cheeks colored, clearly embarrassed by her outburst, and she glanced at Miss Chamberlain, who raised an unimpressed eyebrow.

Hannah grinned at Lady Charlotte. "It is, and I do. Would you like to see him? I call him Tempo."

"May we?" Lady Charlotte may have been the only lady bold enough to speak, but most of the others leaned forward in their seats for a better view.

Hannah set her cup and saucer on the low table in the center of the group. She'd set her reticule on the small couch between herself and Mary in case Miss Chamberlain or her mother favored the small dogs that would make trouble for Tempo.

She lifted the purse onto her lap now and opened it, carefully removing the frog. He blinked blearily around at the group, and she knew she'd woken him.

"Tempo," she said softly in the sing-song tone she'd heard other people use with their pets. She'd used it herself with previous pets, but not with Tempo. It wouldn't do to speak to him like a human in front of this group, however. "These ladies would like to meet you." She cupped him in her hands and held him toward Lady Charlotte.

Hannah's regard for the older girl rose immediately and drastically. Not only did Lady Charlotte not flinch or shriek, as Miss Hopewell on her other side showed every sign of doing if Hannah brought the frog any nearer to her, but she smiled and met Hannah's eyes. "May I touch him?" At Hannah's nod, Lady Charlotte reached out a delicate finger and brushed it lightly along Tempo's mottled back. "He's so smooth!" she exclaimed. "I thought he might be slimy or wet, but he's not."

As if Lady Charlotte's bravery gave permission to the rest, four of the other girls rose and crowded around Hannah, each asking to pet Tempo and barraging her with questions about what he ate and how far he could jump and if she really did carry him everywhere in her pocket. Their enthusiasm made Hannah suddenly worry that Henry's prediction had been right and that wild frogs would suddenly be in fashion.

"I do carry him in my pocket," she admitted, settling Tempo on her lap as the girls returned to their seats to eye the frog from a distance. "But frogs make rather inconvenient pets. They're nocturnal, for one thing, which means they're asleep all day and awake at night. They need to swim regularly or their skin will dry out. And they eat bugs and grubs." That last point got the reaction she'd been hoping for: sounds of mild disgust and wrinkled noses. No need to fear these ladies going out to catch frogs.

"But Lady Hannah," Miss Hopewell said, nostrils flaring as she seemed unable to look away from Tempo, "what possessed you bring it to a *ball*?"

Hannah didn't like the way she'd called Tempo "it." She bit back a retort and said merely, "He seemed bored. I thought he might like to see something new."

Miss Chamberlain and a few others snickered. "You are an original, Lady Hannah." Their hostess's sneer said plainly that she hadn't meant the word as a compliment. "Taking a frog to a ball because you thought it was *bored*. How droll!" She and her hangers-on twittered again. Miss Chamberlain's eyes were cold as she fixed them on Hannah, though her pleasant smile never left her lips. "I suppose you had to do *some*thing to make yourself more interesting to the *ton*, it being your third Season with not a single offer of marriage forthcoming. Being odd has at least gotten you noticed. Tell me, did you choose your pet because his color brings out your eyes?"

Hannah sat frozen for a heartbeat, unable to draw breath. The sentiment was not unexpected, particularly from a cold-hearted vixen like Miss Chamberlain. But she'd sensed Lady Charlotte stiffening in the chair next to her at the comment about multiple Seasons without marriage offers. To be so unfeeling as to spew vitriol that took down innocent bystanders was too far. Hannah opened her mouth to say something cutting, though her mind was alarmingly blank. But she never got a single word out, because Tempo took that moment to jump.

He leapt from her lap to the tea table, landing neatly beside her untouched saucer without even making it rattle. He hopped across the table before she could reach out for him. His strong legs propelled his little body forward into the teacup Miss Chamberlain had set aside, knocking into it so that it toppled, splashing hot tea on her creamy figured muslin skirt. She screeched and jumped to her feet, backing away from the table. The girls on either side of her shrieked and scrambled away as well. Hannah hurried to scoop Tempo up from where he now rested in the middle of Miss Chamberlain's plate of half-eaten pastry.

"Good heavens, I'm sorry—truly, so sorry—please, excuse me!" She grabbed her reticule and hurried from the room, passing a startled footman on her way out the front door.

She hadn't thought to ask for the carriage to be brought round, so she walked around the house toward the mews. As she did, she lifted Tempo up so that she look him in the eye.

"Why?" she asked helplessly. "Why did you have to do that?"

His expression could only be called belligerent, and he glared back at her. "Insult. You."

Hannah sighed. "Of course she insulted me. She's just *like* that. I wasn't surprised or even particularly offended." She set Tempo on her shoulder where he'd ridden the day of the lecture, and he leaned in against her neck. "She can't stand it when anyone else gets more attention than she does."

From behind her, Hannah could hear Mary and Kate calling her name. She turned and waited for them to catch her up. None of them said another word until they'd found their carriage and driver, climbed in, and closed the door.

"You certainly know how to make an exit," Kate said as the vehicle rolled back onto the street.

"Did you see Miss Chamberlain's face?" Mary squeaked. "And Miss Hopewell looked like she might faint!"

CHAPTER 10

The three girls looked at each other and all broke into fits of helpless giggles that lasted until they made the final turn into Berkeley Square. Then, laughter subsiding, Mary peered at Tempo.

"I don't know if you can understand me, Tempo," she said, "but that was brilliant. I'll never forget it."

Hannah and Kate exchanged a look before following Mary out of the carriage.

Inside her room, Hannah set Tempo on her bed and sank down beside him.

"I do appreciate you standing up for me," she said. "I hope I didn't come across as ungrateful. It means a lot that you were offended on my behalf, and I know you were doing what you could to defend my honor. You're sweet like that, aren't you?"

Tempo croaked wordlessly and hopped to perch on her lap. She stroked one finger from the top of his head down his back, again and again, feeling the cool smoothness of his skin. His bulbous eyes closed.

"It's probably best if you don't cause another display like that again, though," she said after a minute. "If Mama thinks that you're uncontrolled or unpredictable, or really if you're poorly behaved in any way, I won't be allowed to carry you with me anymore. She won't stop me from carrying you about the house, but balls and teas and morning calls will be out of the question. I'd hate to have to leave you home."

"I won't. Do it. Again."

Hannah sensed something he wasn't saying. "Unless…"

"Unless. Your. Safety. Is. At risk."

She tilted her head, trying to fill in the gaps in his words. "So you won't jump on a tea table again if a lady insults me, but if Lord Trellion were to corner me on a balcony again, you'd be all over his face like last time?"

Tempo nodded and blinked at her. "Correct."

"Your loyalty is remarkable, Tempo, darling. I don't deserve it. I'm no closer to finding a way to turn you back to yourself."

"You do. Deserve. Because. *You*." He fixed her with the fiercest look a frog had probably ever given. "Not what. You do… Just. You."

Hannah felt a prickling at the back of her eyes and a tightness at her heart. Despite his own concerns, Tempo had somehow still managed to be one of the very few people who saw her as she was and liked her that way.

"Thank you," she managed. She stroked her finger along his back a few more times, swallowing hard and blinking to rid herself of the impending tears. "You deserve better, though. What do you miss most about being human? Perhaps I can do something."

"Awake. Daytime."

Hannah released her breath in a small huff. "I'm afraid I can't do anything about being nocturnal. What else?"

At first she expected him to choose a food, something other than the grubs and bugs he ate daily, but Tempo looked at her long and hard, as if he were sorting through possible answers. Were the things he missed inappropriate to discuss with young ladies? Hannah rejected that notion; Tempo didn't seem the type. More likely, in his incessant thoughtfulness, he wanted to choose an answer that she could help with, so that she wouldn't feel guilty for being unable to. Or maybe he just didn't want to speak his wishes aloud so that he wouldn't get his hopes up only to be dashed.

"Riding," he said at last. "Boxing. Cards."

Hannah studied him. "Oh, dear. I'm afraid I can't do anything at all about boxing—you're not built for it at the moment, and I couldn't possibly take you to a mill."

"No," Tempo agreed.

"I wish I could take you riding," she mused. "I miss it too. But we left my mare at home, and the carriage horses are too tall for me. I don't know if I could find one to let from a public stable?" She frowned. "And I'd have to have someone to go riding with me. Now that Henry's married he's less available for that kind of thing." She bit her lower lip, missing Johnson badly. The only times she'd been riding in town had been with him, on a horse he borrowed for her. He was attentive and thoughtful, he understood her unlike anyone but Henry and Kate, and he'd only gotten better with age.

She bit back a sigh and determined to address the subject of riding later. "What kind of cards?"

"Whist. Quadrille. Any-. Thing."

"I'm afraid I don't know how to play whist, but I could learn. Henry could teach me. I'd bet Kate would like to play too, and I think Mama enjoys the game." Hannah jumped to her feet. "We don't have plans for tomorrow night. I'm going to talk my family into holding our own private card party."

Chapter 11

Nathaniel had had to think hard about what to tell Hannah. When she'd asked what he missed about being human, he'd been overset by visions of holding Hannah's hand in his, of taking her in his arms and stealing kisses on a private balcony. Of course, those things had never happened, so he couldn't *miss* them, per se, but they were the strongest reasons he wanted to be human. Things he missed… He remembered exploring the grounds of Cauldercrest with Hannah and her brothers. Taking Hannah riding, once during her first Season and a few times her second. Sitting across from her at family dinners and laughing together at some joke. Dancing together. She was an infinitely superior dancer, but he had taken any opportunity to be near her.

But he couldn't say any of that. He tried—he'd hoped "family dinners" might be acceptable, or "dancing with you," but the magic must have latched onto his intentions and smothered the words before they reached his mouth. So he resigned himself to acknowledging the third tier of wishes, the things he had done in town on ordinary days. He did very much miss riding and boxing, and maybe they'd provide Hannah with a small clue of his identity, since she knew he liked them, but he hadn't been pining after them by any means.

CHAPTER 11

Her excitement over playing cards endeared her to him further because she was eager to learn a new game solely for his sake.

The next evening, Nathaniel rode on Hannah's shoulder to the library, where they found Henry sitting at a table with a pack of cards.

"You're a whist player, Tempo?" Henry asked, when Hannah had closed the door behind her.

"Yes," Nathaniel said.

Hannah flinched, and he berated himself for croaking so close to her ear.

"He can't hold the cards, so I'll hold them for him. I thought it would be best to learn and practice for a bit with just you before Mama joins us. I can't begin to imagine what she'd say if she knew a frog was playing cards."

Henry explained the rules, and Nathaniel settled into his favorite spot leaning against the curve of Hannah's neck. Henry dealt, then walked Hannah through a trick. Nathaniel could see her cards easily as she held them up.

"What do you think, Tempo? What should I put down?"

Nathaniel hesitated. He wouldn't croak in her ear again, and he could hardly tell her what to do once they were playing for real. How could this possibly work?

"How about this? Tap once for no and twice for yes."

Hannah slowly pointed to each card in turn. Nathaniel tapped with his front foot on her collarbone, and she set down the card he chose.

"You'll have to get faster than that," Henry said, observing with raised brows. "We'll all be tripping over our white beards if we have to wait that long."

"I'll get faster as I get better at the game," Hannah defended herself. She fixed her brother with a challenging glare. "I'm new to this. I'm sure I could rule out some of the cards on my own. Go again."

Hannah did get faster. As Henry talked her through trick after trick, Hannah stopped pointing to all the cards in her hand and only asked Nathaniel to choose between two or three.

"This isn't bad," Hannah said finally, "though I can't see why the game is so popular. The only fun part is seeing if I can guess which card Tempo will choose before he tells me, and that's not an official part of whist."

Henry chuckled. "Let's call in Mother and Father. Then maybe you'll see."

"Are Kate and Mary not playing?"

"It's a four-person game, and Kate wanted to go to bed early this evening."

Henry left to invite the others to play. Hannah whispered, "Are you enjoying yourself?"

Nathaniel tapped twice on her collarbone. Playing cards as a team with Hannah was an entirely different experience, but he was quickly deciding it was his favorite way to play.

The duke and duchess joined them, and Mary tucked herself into an armchair to watch. Henry dealt, and the game was underway. Nathaniel could feel the gradual change in Hannah as the evening went on. Her mother's enthusiasm for the game fed her own, and she made no more comments about the game being uninteresting. Nathaniel had forgotten how much fun it could be to play cards with the Stantons. There had been plenty of rainy days during his visits over the years when they'd all piled into the parlor with hot chocolate and tea, using buttons from Mary's sewing supplies for their wagers. This was the warm, loving, playful family that he had always wanted for himself, and he'd treasured his welcome into their midst.

**

On Monday evening, Hannah and her family drove the short distance to the home of the Miss Lemmons. Mary had spent half the day with Miss Lemmon and Miss Christine, preparing for the musicale that evening. The drawing room was small and cozy. Though the furniture and wallpaper were several years out of style, it was a comfortable room, and fit the small assembly. Hannah took a seat beside Kate, perfectly situated to see Mary at the pianoforte. Tempo sat on her lap. The view would have been better from her shoulder, and he seemed to like sitting there—at least, he'd seemed comfortable enough while they'd played cards the other night, and he'd fallen asleep on her shoulder at the lecture—but he was simply too visible there. She was afraid the sight of him might upset someone. Mrs. Lemmon was notoriously high-strung, and Hannah didn't want to cause trouble.

The three girls had practiced a dozen songs, some on their own, some together. Mary and Miss Christine both played the pianoforte, and Miss Lemmon played the harp. All three sang, sweet and light, and Hannah was enraptured by their harmonies.

The evening ended with refreshments. With a cup of punch in hand, Hannah approached her sister and her friends.

"Lady Hannah!" exclaimed Miss Lemmon. "What did you think? I know you're musical as well."

"I can say with absolute honesty that I've never enjoyed a musicale as much as I've enjoyed this evening," Hannah said. "Your voices blended beautifully."

"You ought to come play with us sometime," Miss Christine insisted. "I found the time practicing to be more fun than the performance."

"More fun for *us*," Miss Lemmon agreed, darting a glance around the room. "The performance is for others."

Hannah wondered if there was a specific "other" that Miss Lemmon was looking for, and what he thought of the performance.

Mary and Mama happily relived the entire evening on the ride home. Kate rested her head against Henry's shoulder. Hannah envied them, having someone to lean on when the day wore down. She stiffened her spine and looked out the window, willing herself not to think about the person she wished would stand by her at the end of the day.

The usual bustle of arriving home dissipated as they all made their way to their rooms for the night. Mrs. Prescott caught Hannah just before she reached the stairs. Hannah jumped and pressed a hand to her heart. "You startled me. I'd thought you'd all be abed by now."

"Soon, my lady," the housekeeper said with a smile. "Monsieur wants to know if there's anything special you'd like him to prepare for dinner for your birthday tomorrow."

In the confusing mix of everything going on this Season, with Kate's pregnancy, Johnson's disappearance, and Tempo's condition, Hannah had nearly forgotten her own birthday. She almost wished she could forget it again—they usually left town about a fortnight after her birthday, returning to the country before London became hot and miserable. Which meant she had two weeks to complete her promise to herself. She hated the idea of giving up on Johnson when he wasn't even present to have a say in the matter, though she supposed his absence could be considered a sign as well. Thinking about letting him go, however, made her stomach turn. She was still horribly worried for him. Maybe she ought to allow herself one more Season to win his affection.

Of course, none of this was relevant to the housekeeper.

"All of Monsieur's dishes are spectacular, so I submit to his choice for dinner, but I would love it if he'd serve ices. His lemon and strawberry ices are my favorites, and I believe he was experimenting with a treacle cream ice?"

Mrs. Prescott's smile warmed. "So I've heard. I'll let him know." She curtsied and bustled away down the dim hallway.

"I know it's not grasshoppers, but I think you'd like strawberry ice," Hannah murmured to Tempo as she climbed the stairs. "Perhaps I can have an extra bowl of it sent up to my room after dinner for you to try."

***

The next morning Hannah was up with the sun. She blinked sleepily, wondering what had woken her. She'd grown used to the sounds of Tempo splashing in the washbasin, and though the sky through her window looked clear and bode well for a lovely day, the sun wasn't high enough yet to make her room overbright. Whatever the cause, awake she was, and awake she would stay. It was her birthday, her one-and-twentieth, and though she told herself she was no longer a child to be so excited about a particular day, she couldn't help swinging her legs over the side of the bed and jumping to her feet with more eagerness than mornings usually warranted.

She dressed in her favorite persimmon morning dress, tied on her apron, and shrugged into a deep brown spencer, as the morning air was chill and damp. Then she braided and pinned her hair somewhat haphazardly before rushing back into the bedroom.

Tempo watched her, his expression unreadable.

"It's a perfect morning to go to Hyde Park," Hannah said. "Would you like to?"

The frog croaked and hopped into her outstretched hands. Hannah slipped him into her apron pocket and took the back stairs two at a time. She left her bonnet and gloves behind. It was too early for anyone fashionable to see her, and today she wanted to feel the breeze. She skipped along the empty streets and into the wide, grassy park. A light fog drifted around her legs as she walked toward the Serpentine. At the edge of the water, she let Tempo down.

"I'll be sitting on that bench over there," she gestured. "Please don't go too far."

Tempo assented and slipped into the water. Hannah took her place on the bench, enjoying the fresh air despite the clammy chill of the fog. Crescendoing birdsong mixed with the chirp of crickets and the croaking of frogs. This deep into Hyde Park, she could easily pretend she was in the country, and that the elegant homes of Mayfair were not only a few minutes' walk away.

Hannah watched the fog begin to burn off. She hadn't seen Tempo in a while. She was just thinking of calling for him to return home when she heard a low croak near her ankle.

"Lady?"

Looking down, she saw her small, olive-green friend looking up at her, a bright yellow buttercup held by the stem in his wide mouth. She lifted the frog up, flower and all. He dropped the buttercup into her hand.

CHAPTER 11

"Birthday. Joy."

Hannah looked from the frog to the flower and back. She thought Tempo was smiling, though there was something about the expression in his eyes that she couldn't read. A smile grew on her own face as she took the flower between her thumb and forefinger and held it up to examine it. It was perfect, a delicate, golden chalice suitable for a tiny fae princess, like in the stories she and Mary had been told in the nursery as children.

"It's beautiful, Tempo, thank you. This is so sweet and thoughtful of you." She tucked the flower over her ear and stroked a finger down the frog's back.

As she settled Tempo back into her apron pocket and began the walk home, she marveled at the unusual friendship they'd developed. Girl and frog, or rather, lady and enchanted gentleman. If they'd both been human and spending this much time together, everyone would say they were practically in each other's pockets. She laughed to herself. That phrase had a whole new meaning when one of them was only three inches long and actually riding in a pocket. But she loved having Tempo around. His sweetness in giving her a gift—even one so small as a flower he picked himself—warmed her heart and brightened her day.

After breakfast with her family, Hannah went with Mama and Kate to call on Lady Sterling. Before she was allowed to leave, of course, Hannah had to change and have her hair dressed properly by one of the maids.

The Countess of Sterling greeted them in the drawing room, welcoming them with a gracious smile. She was a picture of stately elegance, still willowy despite being of an age with Mama. Her rosy golden curls were swept up in a neat chignon, and her blue eyes gleamed with kindness and interest.

"I am glad you could come," she said, gesturing them all to sit. Two other ladies were already present. Hannah recognized Lady York, and the other, a slight woman whose blonde hair was fading to gray, was introduced as Lady Everley. Hannah sat between her mother and Kate on the sofa, resting her reticule on her lap.

"I've heard any number of rumors about events that occurred at my ball last week," Lady Sterling said. "I do hope you can clear them up. I confess, I'm eaten up with curiosity."

Hannah blushed. "I am most heartily sorry for having caused a scene, my lady," she murmured, not quite daring to meet Lady Sterling's eye.

"Oh, stuff." Their hostess waved off the apology. "*You're* not the one who stormed through the ballroom cursing like a sailor. What exactly happened with Lord Trellion?"

"Nothing!" Hannah said quickly. "He… he made some hints that were… less than gentlemanly. My… pet frog took exception to his behavior."

Beside her, Kate raised a gloved hand to hide a smirk. Hannah realized that her explanation did sound a bit ridiculous. The older ladies were all staring at her, slightly befuddled.

"I can easily believe that of Trellion," Lady Sterling said coolly, raising an eyebrow. "His reputation is colorful, to say the least."

"'Took exception'?" Lady Everley repeated. "How do you mean? And could a frog really have an opinion?"

"Tempo—my frog, that is—has proven to be as loyal to me as any faithful hound," Hannah said carefully. "I believe he could sense my distress."

"Yes, but what did he *do*?"

"He jumped at his lordship's face."

Kate failed to stifle her giggle. Hannah fought her own laugh as she remembered Tempo clinging to Trellion's nose, his hind foot braced against the man's lower lip. She managed to hold it down, biting her lip to keep her grin in check.

To her surprise, the older ladies chuckled.

"That would explain the foul language," Lady Sterling said, shaking her head. "I hope it taught him a lesson."

"Do you often carry a frog with you?" Lady York asked.

"Since finding Tempo I do," Hannah acknowledged.

"She's had a soft spot for small animals all her life," Mama said with amusement mixed with longstanding exasperation. "At Cauldercrest she was always rescuing something or other and trying to hide her new pet in the schoolroom." Mama turned slightly to give Hannah a smile before adding, "After the events with Lord Trellion, of course, we're just as glad she has Tempo with her."

"Is he with you now?" Lady Everley asked.

Hannah nodded. "Would you like to see him?"

Lady York looked less than thrilled at the idea, but Lady Sterling said, "He won't jump on us, will he?"

"Oh, no. He's very well-behaved around well-behaved people."

A muffled snort from Kate said that she was thinking of Miss Chamberlain's debacle.

Hannah smirked and opened her reticule to extract the sleeping frog. He squirmed a little, starting to wake up, but she settled him on her lap and murmured softly until he stilled again.

"Hmm," Lady Everley said, leaning forward slightly. "I admit, I imagined him to be rather more impressive."

Hannah smiled down at her little friend. "He's a common frog, *Rana temporaria*. I wouldn't recommend them as pets in general, but he's been a delightful companion."

"Speaking of companions," Lady York jumped in, obviously uncomfortable with amphibians and eager to change the subject, "did you hear about Lady Charlotte's companion, Mrs. Yates?"

And with that, the conversation shifted to the latest *on dit*. Hannah was relieved. She'd been afraid that Lady Sterling would be offended at the idea of a frog attending her ball. And she knew that any censure from them would filter through half the *ton* within days.

After a quarter hour of discussing the foibles of the *beau monde*, Mama asked, "Have any of you heard anything about Nathaniel Johnson, son of Lord Bembry?"

Hannah straightened in her seat, as did Kate beside her. Even Tempo seemed to stiffen the slightest bit where he sat on her lap. Hannah felt two light taps from the frog's front foot.

"I haven't," Lady Sterling said, frowning. "What of him?"

"He disappeared without a word weeks ago," Mama explained, her fingers clenching and releasing each other. "Henry finally heard back from Bembry that Nathaniel isn't at the country house." She shook her head. "I've been worried sick. That young man is family to us."

Tempo tapped Hannah's lap again, one-two, and she moved to stroke a finger along his back. She didn't know why he'd woken up, but he ought to keep sleeping.

Lady Everley reached over and rested a comforting hand atop Mama's. "If I hear even a whisper about him, I'll let you know immediately."

The other two ladies murmured their agreement. Mama thanked them, and Hannah sank back, deflated. How could a man of six-and-twenty simply vanish without a trace?

As Hannah lost herself in gloomy thoughts, the conversation moved on without her. She jerked back to the present as she heard Kate speak.

"Yes, a practicing magician. I've been doing magic all my life, but there's one spell I can't get a handle on, and I was hoping to find someone who could help me with it."

Hannah held her breath as she waited to hear what they'd say.

"It's a shame Eleanor and James aren't in town," Lady Everley said to Lady Sterling, who nodded. She turned back to Kate. "My niece Eleanor designs her own spells, and her husband James was a magician for the Royal Navy. But they didn't come this Season."

Lady York listed off a few names, and Hannah committed them to memory. She could tell by the slightly absent look on Kate's face that her friend was memorizing them too. Then her ladyship said, "What about the Royal Magic Library? Have you looked there?"

"No," Kate said. "I didn't know it was open to the public."

"To a degree," Lady York hedged. "It's not available to just any common magician, but they should give you no trouble, with your connections."

"If you don't find what you need," Lady Everley offered, "come to me, and I'll give you Eleanor's direction so you can write to her."

Kate thanked them, and after a few more minutes of pleasantries, their visit ended. Back at home, Kate and Hannah huddled in the entrance hall for a moment after Mama had gone upstairs.

"I'll go to the library tomorrow," Kate said. "Since I doubt they'll allow me to take any books home, do you think Tempo might come along with me? That way if I find a spell, I can try it right away."

"I'll ask him. I can't imagine he'll refuse."

Making plans for the next morning, the two girls climbed the stairs together before separating to go to their rooms to change.

Chapter 12

Nathaniel had spent half the night trying to figure out what to give Hannah for her birthday. If he hadn't lost track of time since becoming a frog, he'd probably have wasted even more time on the fruitless puzzle. Getting her a proper gift was impossible without outside help. Acquiring outside help meant telling someone who he was, and that was proving equally impossible.

So he'd given her a buttercup, the only thing he could get on his own that would show even the tiniest bit that he cared.

It was woefully insufficient, but it was something. Hannah had held a special place in his heart since his mother died. Lady Bembry had been the only person in his childhood to show him affection, and Hannah's simple hug after her loss had meant the world to him. Since then he'd always remembered her birthday. He'd remembered Mary's too, to avoid showing blatant favoritism. The one benefit of his increasingly painful position as honorary brother was that he could give gifts without adhering to rules of propriety. A gentleman could only give a lady gifts of flowers, candy, or books, unless they were betrothed or family. But for Hannah's birthday two years ago, during her first Season, Nathaniel had given her an amber pendant, and no one had said a word against it.

And for this birthday, when she came of age: a buttercup.

He'd been asleep by the time she finished breakfast and had dressed to go out. He'd groggily heard her mention that they were calling on Lady Sterling as she tucked him into her reticule and had been vaguely aware of voices and light as she'd taken him from the bag. He'd woken almost fully when he'd heard his real name, and he'd tried to pass Hannah a coded message as the duchess spoke. Two taps. *Yes. Yes, I have news of Nathaniel Johnson. Yes, yes, I'm here.*

Tap-tap.

But Hannah had missed his message, or else she hadn't felt them, and she'd stroked his back until he succumbed again to his nocturnal instincts and dozed off.

When Nathaniel woke again, they were back in Hannah's room. She'd already divested herself of bonnet, gloves, and spencer. Her reticule sat open on a chair, and she encouraged him to jump out and up to the basin. He did, splashing into the water and enjoying a swim before settling back onto his pillow to sleep the rest of the afternoon.

Hannah was gone when he woke again. The evening sky beyond the window grew steadily dimmer. Nathaniel wished he could be downstairs for her birthday dinner, but Alice had banned frogs from the table.

Full dark had fallen when Hannah returned to her room. She came with a lit candle, which she used to light two others. The flickering candlelight obscured the exact shade of Hannah's green dress, but it made her neck and semi-exposed shoulders glow like marble. She wore no jewelry except a small teardrop of amber nestled at her throat. Nathaniel's heart performed uncomfortable acrobatics as he recognized the pendant he'd given her.

CHAPTER 12

"Good. Dinner?" he choked out, his eyes fixed on the pendant.

"Very," she said. "Monsieur never disappoints. I've asked for a bowl of strawberry ice to be sent up so you can try it." Hannah smiled, but it didn't reach her eyes. She kept her voice bright, however, as she said, "Look at the bonnet Mary gave me." She held up an elegant creation of silk flowers and ribbons. "She took one several years out of style and made it up new, and I really think it's nicer than any you'd see on Bond Street."

"Very. Nice," Nathaniel said, wondering what emotions she was trying to hide.

"Henry and Kate gave me a new set of paints," she went on. "And Daniel sent me a book about wildflowers." She held up the book in question before setting it on the bed to read later. Hannah sighed then, so faintly that he'd have missed it if he hadn't been watching her so closely.

"Something. Wrong?"

"No, of course not," she said quickly. "It was a lovely day, and I have the most wonderful family. And Kate has a new plan for finding the spell. I forgot to mention—could you go to the Royal Magic Library with her tomorrow? She was hoping to have you nearby if she finds a spell worth trying."

"Yes." He'd miss being with Hannah, but he needed to be human again, and soon.

"Excellent."

Hannah left the room, returning later in her dressing gown, with her hair long and loose down her back. She blew out two of the candles and brought the third to her bedside table. Once under the blankets, she opened the wildflower book from Daniel. Nathaniel hopped onto the bed to sit at her shoulder, nestled in the waves of her hair, and look at the book with her.

After several silent minutes spent staring at the same page, Nathaniel croaked, "Lady?"

"Hmm?"

"Thinking?"

Hannah's brow furrowed slightly, and she looked at him. Her freckles had darkened slightly, but were still only a trace of what he remembered of her as a girl. "Pardon?"

"Not. Turning. Pages," Nathaniel pointed out. "Thinking?"

"Oh," Hannah glanced back at the book, chagrinned. "Sorry, I'm afraid my mind did wander off." She turned to the next page, again leaving it open for longer than she would normally.

"Tell me. What's. Wrong?"

Hannah sighed. "I don't know why I bothered trying to hide it from you, Tempo. You know me better than that by now, don't you? It's just… It's Johnson. He's still missing, and his father doesn't know where he is any more than we do." She fell silent.

"Worried?" Could he use this opportunity to give her a hint she couldn't miss?

"Yes, but it's also… It's my birthday, you know, and Johnson hasn't missed a single birthday since, well, almost since I've known him. He always comes to dinner, and even if he can't come, he sends a letter and a gift. Not that I think I need more gifts, but… he's never forgotten before."

"Didn't. Forget," Nathaniel protested. He couldn't let Hannah think she'd slipped his mind.

Hannah smiled kindly at him. "No, Tempo, *you* didn't forget. You were the first to wish me joy on my birthday this morning, and it was the most meaningful gift I received." She looked at the tiny buttercup which she'd placed in a brown glass vial of water on her bedside table. Closing the book, she laid it next to the vial with the flower and blew out the candle. "I don't think I'll read any more tonight. I just can't concentrate."

This was his last chance for today. He had to try again. "Lady," he said. What could he tell her? "Necklace."

Hannah's hand went to her throat, where the amber pendant had rested until she'd taken it off when readying for bed.

"From—" The magic stopped him before he could say "me." He'd gotten farther than any previous attempt, but it wasn't enough.

"Johnson gave it to me two birthdays ago," Hannah said with a sad, tired smile.

Nathaniel, still struggling to get a word out, tapped his chest—or what passed for one on a frog—with one front foot. *I did. It was me.*

But Hannah didn't see it. She was already rolling to face away from him. "Goodnight, Tempo," she mumbled.

Nathaniel stared at the back of her head, at the curve of her shoulders, moving softly with her breathing. Gradually, her breathing slowed, and Nathaniel slumped. He wanted her to stay awake so that he could try again to tell her his truth, never mind the humiliation he'd face when she knew. But he also wanted her to sleep, to rest after her disappointing day. She was disappointed because of *him*, because he wasn't there, because he'd idiotically gotten into a duel with a magician. He'd never felt so small, even as a three-inch frog. He'd let Hannah down.

Nathaniel hopped silently back to his pillow beside the water basin and sulked in the dark.

Chapter 13

On Monday morning, following his breakfast in the garden and the family's breakfast, Nathaniel jumped into Hannah's open reticule. She cinched it shut, saying, "Don't worry about a thing, Tempo. Kate will take good care of you. I'll see you tonight."

"Tonight. Lady," he agreed. He trusted Kate. Hannah couldn't know that Nathaniel had met Kate a handful of times before becoming a frog. His best friend's wife was sweet, intelligent, and unaffected. She was beloved by the entire Stanton family, and by extension, himself.

Though the inside of the reticule was dark, Nathaniel stayed awake and listening as Hannah carried him downstairs to meet Kate. The reticule changed hands, and he heard Kate promise not to let him go more than a couple of hours without water. More movement, and then some jostling as Kate was handed into the coach. He could feel the rumble as the conveyance rolled off. The motion lulled him, and as it had passed the time he ought to be asleep, he began to doze. He couldn't tell how far they'd come when he was jostled again as the carriage stopped and Kate climbed out.

"Here we are," Kate said softly. "The Royal Magic Library." The mouth of the reticule opened slightly. "Would you like to see?"

Nathaniel maneuvered so that his head poked through the opening. The building before them was about the size of two Mayfair townhouses, three stories tall, with arched windows and a line of graceful columns. The golden stone of the building glowed in the late morning light. Something was carved in relief above the door, but he couldn't make it out. Kate swept up the steps and nodded graciously to the footman who opened the door for her. Just inside, a small, mousy man with a quizzing glass bustled over and informed her that the library wasn't open to visitors.

"Is it not?" Kate asked. "I was told that the Magic Library was open to all magicians of status."

"To serious magicians, yes," the man blustered.

Nathaniel considered jumping on the man, who obviously thought that because of Kate's age and gender that she didn't deserve access to the books inside.

But Kate's answer stopped him. "Are you implying that I'm not a serious magician? Or that I'm of a low class?" She held out one hand and a flame ignited in her gloved palm without a spoken word. The flame vanished, replaced by a rushing wind, which stopped just as silently. Kate raised an eyebrow at him. "I assure you, I am a magician. If universities were open to female students, I could easily earn a place."

"But, miss, I assure you—"

"Ah, forgive me, I haven't introduced myself," Kate said, smiling politely. "Mrs. Catherine Stanton, wife of Lord Henry Stanton, eldest son and heir to the Duke of Caulder."

The man blanched, and his quizzing glass trembled. "Even so, my lady, I cannot simply—"

Kate sighed. "Look, I've tried being polite, but you're being obstinate and rude. I will get inside this library. There's a spell I need to find, and I *will* find it. You can either let me in now, or I can go home to Berkeley Square and inform my father-in-law, the Duke of Caulder, that you excluded me. He'll come back with me tomorrow—irritated, I'm sure, that he had to interrupt his own plans to deal with a puffed-up doorkeeper—and you will let me in then." She fixed him with a sharp glare. "Which will it be, sir?"

The mousy librarian stepped back and waved her through. Kate sailed past him, head high. Once out of earshot, she let out her breath in a huff of silent laughter.

"I'm getting better at acting like a duchess," she whispered. "I couldn't have done that a year ago. Maybe by the time I'm actually a duchess I'll be able to hold my own."

"I'm. Impressed."

Kate grinned down at him. "Let's go find that book."

The library was laid out in a series of small, interconnected rooms. They all blended together: floor-to-ceiling bookshelves, narrow windows, tables and chairs of golden wood and burgundy leather. Only the books were different. Each room seemed to have a theme, though Nathaniel knew so little about magic that the designations were meaningless. After skimming shelves in the first floor and half of the second, Kate found titles that looked promising. She set the open reticule on a table and began pulling books off the shelf. Nathaniel hopped out of the reticule to sit in the warmth of the watered-down sunlight filtering through the nearest window and watch. Once Kate had a stack of five or six thick tomes, she settled into a chair and began to page through them.

Nathaniel found the atmosphere of the Royal Magic Library to be just as soporific as that of the Bodleian Library at Oxford,

CHAPTER 13

where he'd nodded off more than once as a student. Here, with nothing to occupy him and only Kate's quiet swish of pages to break the silence, he soon sank into a sound sleep. Occasionally, as if from a great distance, he heard Kate murmur something like, "Perhaps volume two," or, disgusted, "One would think a book about metamorphosis would have *some*thing useful to say."

He woke to Kate tapping him lightly on the back with one finger. "It's time to go home, Tempo. Can you hop back into the reticule, or shall I lift you?"

He blinked and hopped himself back into the purse, but not before noticing the stacks and stacks of books that Kate had left out for the librarians to shelve. There had to be at least thirty. Had she paged through that many? Gratitude flared within him at how much time and effort she was putting into this search.

"Thanks. Kate," he said. "I owe. You. For your. 'Elp."

"Nonsense." He could hear the smile in her voice, though she'd tightened the strings of the reticule already. "I'd do anything for Hannah or her friends, and I know how helpless it feels to be at the mercy of unwanted magic."

***

Hannah felt strangely lonely after handing Tempo off to Kate and watching them leave. She'd wanted to go with Kate to the library, but Mama had already claimed her morning. There would be callers, as there were most days, and having Mary out in society hadn't distracted Mama from finding a match for Hannah. She envied Kate, who, being already married, had the time and freedom to do what she liked.

Mary was upstairs practicing the pianoforte, but Hannah wasn't in a musical mood, so she sat in the drawing room with the book Daniel had given her. Before she could read more than a page or two—the same ones she'd stalled over with Tempo last night—Mama joined her on the sofa.

"Hannah, dear, I've been thinking."

Hannah closed the book, marking her page with a ribbon, and looked at her mother quizzically.

"I know that in the past we left town a fortnight after your birthday, but I think we ought to go early this year, given Kate's condition. She'd really be much better off in her own home in the country."

Hannah frowned. "How soon were you thinking?"

"A week, or sooner if we can manage it. She's been looking peaked each evening, and I'm truly afraid the city air and endless crowds are wearing on her too much."

Hannah looked down at her book, forcing her fingers to relax their grip. Being at home in the country *would* be good for her friend, but that didn't stop the panic that surged through her. A week or less to find a cure for Tempo? A week or less before she had to give up Johnson, or else break her promise to herself? And Johnson was still missing! She took a long, slow breath. There wasn't now, nor had there been, anything they could do for Johnson. Having an end date to their time in London didn't change that, and whenever he did turn up, he knew where to find them at Cauldercrest. But that only mollified *one* of her concerns. It didn't help Tempo a jot.

Mama was talking again, and Hannah wrenched her attention back.

"You look distressed, dear. Is there... someone you're loath to leave so soon?"

CHAPTER 13

What could Hannah say? No, none of her suitors were causing this reluctance to leave town. She gave her head a tiny shake.

"Several gentlemen have been quite attentive, and I wondered if one of them had caught your eye?"

Hannah shook her head again.

"We could make alternate arrangements, you know. Henry and Kate could go home without us. Or—Papa will be staying until Parliament is finished later this summer, so you could stay here with him, and I'm sure Lady Sterling or Lady Yorke would be happy to chaperone you…?"

If she hadn't still been panicking, Hannah might have found it funny how hopeful Mama sounded.

"Or, you know, if you come to an agreement within the next few days, you could write each other. We could even host a house party at Cauldercrest."

And Mama was off, talking through the logistics of this proposed party. Hannah briefly considered remaining in town and extending her Season, but she couldn't find a spell for Tempo without Kate, so it would do no good to stay behind. It wouldn't change anything for Johnson, and it would only delay the inevitable regarding her feelings for him. They might as well all go home together. But as Mama patted her hand and left to discuss travel arrangements with Mrs. Prescott, Hannah prayed that Kate and Tempo would find the spell they needed today, and even more fervently that Johnson would turn up soon.

***

By the time they arrived home and Nathaniel had been given

back into Hannah's care, it was already late in the afternoon. He had a good swim, or as good as he could manage in the small basin, while Hannah ate an early dinner before dressing for the concert. Her dress for tonight was a bright aqua, bolder than the usual pastels worn by debutantes, but it suited her. It was trimmed with gold cord, and the matching sash—with sewn-in pocket—was shot with gold thread. Nathaniel had never been one to care much for fashion, especially ladies' fashion, but he couldn't help noticing every detail about Hannah. He could have stared at her all night.

But Hannah crossed the room in three quick strides, saying, "We don't want to be late. It's our box, of course, so we'll have seats no matter when we arrive, but Vivaldi is so lovely that I don't want Kate to miss a minute." She scooped him up gently and tucked him into her sash pocket.

After all that Kate had done for him, Nathaniel didn't want her to miss out either.

At the theater, Hannah let him out of her pocket to sit on her lap. From here he could see the candlelight gleaming on the orchestra on stage, the brightly clothed patrons in the opposite boxes, and the tops of the heads of the general audience below. Kate sat between Henry and Hannah, looking around excitedly.

"You didn't tell me that coming to the theater was half the fun," she said, leaning over to talk to Hannah. "Look at everyone!"

"I would have brought you last season if Henry had only listened to my advice and eloped with you," Hannah teased.

Kate blushed but was spared answering by the opening bars of music.

The orchestra was top-notch. Nathaniel could tell that even with no expertise in music. He let the sound dance over him, enjoying himself though concerts had never been his favorite entertainment. He preferred more active pursuits. When he did listen to music, he preferred small, intimate drawing room performances. Mary and Hannah both played very well, and he'd had ample opportunity to listen over the years as they practiced and improved.

One of Hannah's fingers absently began to stroke along his head and down his back. Even through the silk glove, he could feel her warmth. He relaxed instantly, sinking into a kind of glorious stupor. If attending concerts could always mean being this close to Hannah, he'd go every day.

Nathaniel was roused from his dreamy state at intermission. Their box received a steady stream of visitors. Captain Franklin and Lord Kerr each stopped to pay their respects to Hannah and petition her for a dance at Almack's on Wednesday. Lady Haseltine and her daughter spoke for several minutes with Kate and Hannah about the music. Kate gushed with praise, which Hannah seconded. Lady Haseltine had a slight complaint about the second violin, but she admitted it was a delightful performance.

Mr. Wilson joined them for the last few minutes of intermission. He studied Nathaniel with interest. Nathaniel suspected the man hadn't seen many frogs this close before, and never one so at ease around people. Even so, he bristled at the man's evaluation. Wilson and Hannah debated the differences between the common frog, of which Nathaniel served as an example, and the common toad, or *Bufo bufo*, a Latin name that Hannah couldn't say without a slight and adorable giggle. Wilson seemed affected by her giggle too, turning a few degrees toward her, his smile growing warmer. Jealousy seeped through Nathaniel, and he glared at Wilson.

He'd promised Hannah not to cause any more scenes, and he could offer no justification, but the impulse to leap at the man's face and jab a sticky, webbed foot in his eye was almost unbearable.

The music began again, but Wilson remained. He leaned over to murmur something to Hannah about the composition. She smiled and answered. Nathaniel glowered.

When the concert finally ended, Wilson gave Nathaniel an appraising look. "I've never seen a frog so quiet, loyal, or well-behaved," he said. "If they're all like yours, they'll become more popular than small dogs." He frowned. "But I don't think your Tempo likes me."

"Why ever not?" Hannah asked. Nathaniel could feel her gaze on him.

"He's been glaring at me ever since I sat down," Wilson said with a bemused chuckle. "I'm not an expert at reading frog expressions, but I get a rather strong feeling that he wishes me gone."

Hannah lifted Nathaniel so that she could look at his face. He blinked at her innocently.

"I'm sure that's not true," Hannah said, slipping him back into her sash pocket. "Tempo gets along with everyone."

"Except Trellion," Wilson pointed out.

"And Miss Chamberlain," Kate added, joining the conversation.

"Very well, *nearly* everyone," Hannah corrected. "He's probably bored and ready for a swim."

They moved to leave. Nathaniel could hear Henry and Kate talking in front of Hannah, so Hannah and Wilson must be following them out of the box.

Wilson's voice came quiet and close, as if he were leaning in.

CHAPTER 13

"It was a pleasure to see you tonight, Lady Hannah. Would you do me the honor of driving in the park with me tomorrow?"

"I'd love to," she said.

Nathaniel's stomach dropped like a stone. Hannah wanted to spend time alone with Wilson. The knowledge ate at him like a canker. He had no right to be jealous. Hannah didn't belong to him. He'd never dared to put himself forward as a suitor. If he'd tried to court her and she wasn't interested, their friendship would have become strained and awkward, and he'd valued his position in their family too much to risk losing it. Henry was like a brother to him, and his parents had become parents to Nathaniel, too, in the absence of his own. Besides, he'd heard Hannah state outright several times over the previous Seasons that she wouldn't marry unless she was over head and ears in love. He'd figured he had time to watch and wait, alert to any sign that her affection for him ranked higher than merely a fondness for Henry's best friend.

He'd only recently decided not to let that fear hold him back any longer. As soon as he was human again, he meant to pursue her, no matter what.

Only now he feared he was too late. As the carriage rolled homeward, he berated himself. He shouldn't have waited, shouldn't have given her time to fall in love with someone else. He should have spoken to her father the very night of her coming-out ball, the night he'd realized that little Hannah had grown up and he couldn't imagine marrying anyone else.

Nathaniel fought against despair. Wilson had caught her attention, and as a frog he could do nothing to stop it. He needed Kate to find the spell and release him before Wilson proposed. Not only did he need to be human to win Hannah's heart, he knew that living as her pet while she was romanced by Wilson would utterly destroy him.

Hannah was quiet as she prepared for bed. Nathaniel couldn't read her expression in the dim candlelight, and he couldn't bear her silence.

"Drive. Wilson?"

"Hmm? Oh, yes, I'm going driving with Mr. Wilson tomorrow. I believe he has a charming curricle, and the weather is supposed to be fine." She trailed off, her mind seeming to wander back to wherever it had been. After a moment, she looked at Nathaniel. "You don't dislike him, do you?"

Prior to his pursuit of Hannah, Nathaniel would have called Wilson a fine fellow, but lately there could be no denying that he disliked him immensely. But he grudgingly choked out, "Good. Sort."

"He is a good sort of man," she agreed. "I used to think him a frightful bore, but he's much more engaging now that we've found a subject of common interest. Though, really, how he could think *Bufo bufo* and *Rana temporaria* anything alike is preposterous." She smiled slightly, and Nathaniel hoped her lightened mood was only because she found the common toad's name ridiculous and not because of any fond memories of conversing with Wilson.

"Franklin?" Nathaniel asked. "Kerr?" He mentally kicked himself for torturing himself with a discussion of more of her suitors, but he had to know.

Hannah raised one shoulder in a halfhearted shrug. "They're both very pleasant, and I enjoy dancing with them. I don't think either has any real designs on me, and I'd refuse them if they did offer." She climbed into bed and blew out the candle.

She fell silent, and Nathaniel stewed silently. Franklin and

Kerr might be out of the running, but Wilson was still a contender.

After a few minutes, when Nathaniel had assumed Hannah was very nearly asleep, she said, "Do you want to come driving with us tomorrow, Tempo? You haven't gotten to ride in a curricle yet, I don't think."

Silently witnessing a private conversation between Hannah and Wilson sounded like the worst kind of torment imaginable.

"Go with. Kate," he croaked. His fear of losing Hannah superseded everything, even his worry over losing his inheritance. He needed to break the curse. Now. "Human. Again."

"Right. Of course."

Her voice was too muffled for him to tell, but was there a chance she sounded… disappointed? Did she want him to come with her for her own sake rather than his? Had she missed him when he was with Kate for the day?

Nathaniel shook himself and slipped into the basin with a small plop. Regardless of how she felt, he'd missed her today, but time was running out, and Kate was his only hope.

Chapter 14

Kate had already been gone an hour by the time Mr. Wilson was announced. That hour had given Hannah plenty of time to regret accepting his offer of a drive. As mild as the day was, with rain unlikely until later, and as much as she enjoyed driving through Hyde Park, she wished she'd gone with Kate instead. Guilt gnawed at her. She'd allowed—persuaded, obliged, compelled—her sister-in-law to take on the enormous task of returning Tempo to his human form, while she did what? She saw to the frog's daily needs, but those were minimal. She carried him around with her like a toy, a mascot, showing him off to the nosier members of the *ton*. But what good had she actually done him? His simple words last night had cut her deeply because the more she'd enjoyed his presence and friendship, the more she'd forgotten that he was trapped in an inconvenient and undesirable form. No man would want to be carried around in a lady's pocket to tedious social calls and teas. She liked having him with her, liked knowing she had a loyal friend at her side no matter how many catty ladies made snide comments. But that wasn't fair to him.

Human. Again.

That was the goal. It always had been.

CHAPTER 14

So Hannah wished now that she'd dropped all social obligations to go with Kate on her search for the spell. Hannah only knew the very basics of magic, having no talent for it herself, but she could imagine how many books there were to search through, if men had been writing treatises on the subject since Aristotle and Socrates. She could at least show Kate anything she thought might refer to the problem at hand and see if Kate found it promising.

Tomorrow, she promised herself. They still had another couple of days before they would leave town, and she'd spend every available hour at the library. She couldn't back out of her commitment to Mr. Wilson, but nothing would keep her from accompanying Kate tomorrow.

Mr. Wilson arrived. Hannah was prepared, needing only a moment to don her bonnet and gloves before she accepted his offered arm. His curricle was an elegant little vehicle, and his matched grays were as fine a pair as Hannah had seen. He handed her up and joined her on the seat, taking the reins and guiding the horses into the street.

"Have you not brought Tempo today?" he asked, glancing at her. "If he's in a pocket, you ought to let him out to enjoy the sun."

"No," Hannah said, forcing a smile. He had no way to know that her frog was a sore subject at the moment. "He's spending the morning with Kate."

"Is he? I had thought he went with you everywhere."

"He often does, but a drive through the park is less conducive to his daily sleep."

Mr. Wilson murmured something understanding about the inconveniences of a nocturnal pet.

Hannah wanted to roll her eyes, take the reins, and rush

across town toward the Royal Magic Library. She could no longer refer to Tempo as a pet, even for the sensibilities of the *ton*. He wasn't a pet. He shouldn't even be a frog.

She controlled her impulses, however, and was grateful when they rolled into Hyde Park for an easy change of subject. She exclaimed over the flowers and the late-blossoming hawthorn trees. They compared favorites: Mr. Wilson was inordinately fond of cherry blossoms, which had gone by weeks ago. Hannah liked them as well, but she found the simple beauty of the buttercup to be brightly charming, though a certain birthday gift might have influenced her opinion. The drive, though slow due to the crush of vehicles on the path enjoying the same scenery and opportunity to greet acquaintance, passed in easy, pleasant conversation. They had turned toward Berkeley Square again when Mr. Wilson turned slightly toward her, his green eyes flicking from the road ahead to meet hers.

"You're a remarkable young lady, you know. I can honestly say I've never met anyone like you, such a blend of beauty, intelligence, and sweetness. You're the first woman I've ever thought I might be able to fall in love with. Would you allow me to court you in earnest to see if we might make each other happy?"

Hannah stared at him, a blush spreading across her cheeks. She appreciated the request, that he'd asked to pursue her rather than going straight to her father to offer for her hand. It was exactly the sort of logical, practical idea she would expect from him. She did like him, and she was beginning to consider him a friend rather than a mere acquaintance. She hadn't thought him deadly dull since they found their shared interest in natural science.

But she couldn't love him. The firm conviction of this smote her as she studied his countenance. She'd hoped, briefly, that maybe he would be the one to help her get over her feelings for Johnson, but it was clear now. No matter how much time they spent together, how often he came to tea or they danced at a ball or he drove her through the park, her feelings wouldn't change. He could never hold a candle to the tall, sandy-haired young man who'd been missing half the season, the boy who'd stolen her heart the day he'd taught her to catch tadpoles.

She'd never stopped loving Johnson, and she doubted she ever could. He was thoughtful and respectful, witty and engaging. He *saw* her, really saw her, and listened to her too. And he never made her feel odd or off-putting. He'd always accepted her as she was, pets and all. What had started as a childish infatuation had deepened and grown roots until she could no more remove her attachment to Johnson than she could cut out her own heart. Her promise to herself at the beginning of the Season had been naïve and misguided. She simply couldn't give him up.

She sighed.

"I'm honored," she said quietly, "and flattered that you think so highly of me. I'm most grateful for your friendship, but I'm afraid my heart isn't available to be won. It has belonged elsewhere for a very long time. I'm sorry."

Mr. Wilson nodded, frowning slightly. He didn't speak or look at her again until he pulled up in front of the house. Then he faced her again. "I hope he knows how lucky he is," he said, his gaze solemn. "Can we remain friends?"

"I'd like that very much."

He jumped down from the curricle and lifted her down, walking her to the front door and bowing to kiss her hand. Hannah paused halfway through the open door, turning to look back at his retreating curricle. She had expected the pleasant ride. She hadn't expected the life-shaking revelation that she loved Johnson with her whole heart and soul.

***

Nathaniel woke up surrounded by stacks of books. He blinked as Kate neatened the stacks from the disorganized heaps she'd made as she cast aside each tome. There had to be nearly fifty books on the table, leaving very little space left for him, the reticule, and the book Kate had left open.

"Sorry. Kate." He'd tried to help. It had taken some work to turn the pages, but he'd done it. But he'd only made it through a dozen or so pages before he'd fallen asleep.

"Don't be," Kate said. "You're nocturnal. You needed sleep."

"You need. Sleep." Kate looked paler than usual, her shoulders sagged, and her eyes were tired.

"Yes," she sighed. "I probably should have stopped an hour or two ago, but we have so little time left, and I kept thinking that the spell I needed would be on the next page, in the next book…" She waved vaguely at the stacks of books around him. "I found something that might work, though. Shall we try it?"

"If you. Think you. Can."

Kate shrugged. "It won't take any energy at all if it doesn't work, and if it does, you can make sure I get home to rest and eat. Agreed?"

"Agreed." He'd have promised a great deal more to be back in his body again.

She sat up tall, making an odd shape with her fingers before holding it over him. The word she spoke sounded like utter gibberish, just like the one she'd tried the first day she'd met him as a frog. Nothing happened. Kate slumped back in her chair.

"Sorry, Tempo. I thought that one might do it."

"Thank you. For. Trying."

She sighed and nodded, then motioned for him to hop into the reticule. She only pulled the strings half closed, so that if he wanted, he could stick his head out. He'd found that the swinging of the bag while walking made him motion sick if he rode that way, but he appreciated the option.

He recognized the mousy librarian's voice as they approached the main doors, speaking to someone else so that he couldn't catch any words at all until they were close, and then only snatches were clear.

"…honored by your patronage, Your Grace…. Harborough."

Nathaniel had heard the name before, but couldn't place it. He didn't think he'd met the Duke of Harborough and briefly wondered why he hadn't. Kate gasped. She hurried forward through the doors, and Nathaniel struggled into the opening of the reticule so he could see what had startled her.

"Pardon me!" she called, hurrying down the steps after an elegant couple dressed in the first stare of fashion. They stopped at the bottom and turned, surprised.

Kate paused in front of them, out of breath. "Forgive me, Your Graces, but did I hear the librarian call you Harborough?"

The gentleman, a tall figure with tanned skin, medium brown hair, and gray eyes, frowned. "I am he, but I don't believe I've had the pleasure of your acquaintance."

"No, you haven't," Kate said, pulling herself together. "But did you once find a spell for Lord Henry Stanton's friend, Miss Whitmer?"

Comprehension dawned on the duke's face, and his expression lightened. "Ah, I did, yes. And you, I'm guessing, are Miss Whitmer?"

Kate blushed. "Mrs. Stanton, now."

The woman on Harborough's arm beamed. "Congratulations."

Kate grinned at her. "Thank you."

Harborough cleared his throat. "It seems we ought to have a proper introduction. I am Thomas Hughes, Duke of Harborough, and this is my wife, Isabelle."

"Call me Belle," the duchess said. Nathaniel didn't recognize her either. She couldn't have been more than three-and-twenty, and she was striking, with dark hair, dark eyes, and a disarming smile.

"Kate," Kate said, reaching out to shake her hand.

"Was there something we can do for you, Kate?" Belle asked.

"Actually, yes. I'm having trouble finding another spell, and I don't know who else to ask. I have searched dozens—probably hundreds—of books to no avail."

"What is the spell for?"

Kate looked down at Nathaniel, and when she saw his head poking out of the reticule, she slowly lifted the bag. "This frog is supposed to be human," she said. Nathaniel could feel all eyes on him. He blinked back at them. "He got into a misguided duel with a magician when they were both in their cups."

If Nathaniel could have blushed, he would have. Nothing like having your own stupidity announced to the world.

"Poor thing!" Belle exclaimed. "Who is he?"

"He can't tell us."

"Bad luck." Harborough grimaced. "You've tried the reversal spell I sent?"

Kate nodded. "It didn't work."

"I can't think of any right off, but I'll see what I can find."

Belle looked thoughtful. "Could the solution be something other than a spell?"

"What do you mean?" Kate asked.

But Belle was looking at her husband, and a whole conversation seemed to pass in that look. "It worked for us."

"But that was a Faerie spell."

"Even so."

Harborough shrugged. "It couldn't hurt."

Belle turned back to Kate. "Perhaps if a lady kisses him and promises to marry him, the spell will break." She looked at Nathaniel. "Being in love would help, but sincerity may be enough."

Kate frowned. "You really think that would work?"

Belle smiled and repeated, "It worked for us." Kate's blue eyes widened, and the duchess laughed. "Come to tea sometime, and I'll tell you all about it. I expect you have a story worth telling yourself."

Nathaniel didn't hear the rest of the conversation. The ladies exchanged a few more pleasantries before they parted ways, but Nathaniel sank back into the obscurity of the reticule, his ears ringing and mind numb. Could the solution to his amphibious condition truly be the thing he wanted most in the world? Would Hannah even do it? She'd touched his slick, wet skin with her bare hands without flinching, but would kissing it be a step too far?

In the carriage, Kate murmured, "*That's* something to consider, isn't it?" She didn't need to explain what she meant; she was obviously thinking the same thing he was. "Will you ask her?"

Nathaniel croaked noncommittally. He wanted to marry

Hannah, but he wanted to propose as a human, not as a frog. It was a huge request—a lifetime commitment, and to a mysterious stranger, as none of his attempts to reveal his identity had worked. It would almost be worse if she knew who he was. For Tempo, Hannah might feel obligated to accept his offer just to turn him back. For Johnson, valued and missed by their whole family, she would absolutely agree because she had the sweetest heart in the world. But he couldn't force her hand like that. She needed to be free to choose whom she liked, no strings attached. Even if it meant he would have to hide in the park or find someone else willing to take in a frog after Hannah chose Wilson.

"Too much. To ask," he said at last. But he couldn't stop thinking about it.

Kate didn't argue, and soon they pulled up at the house. As soon as Kate stepped inside, she was called into the drawing room. Hannah met her at the door, asking softly, "Any luck?"

Nathaniel assumed Kate shook her head, because she handed Hannah the reticule without a word. Alice bustled over then and began to fuss over Kate.

"Where have you been all day? You're so pale! You must come and have a rest before dinner. What is Henry thinking, letting you go off on your own for so long in your condition? I'll have a word with him tonight, to be sure. It's a good thing we're leaving in a few days…" Her voice receded, out of the drawing room and down the hall, punctuated by quiet protests from Kate that she was fine, merely tired, and that Henry was taking excellent care of her.

Hannah, meanwhile, opened the reticule and reached in for him. Her expression was filled with sympathy and remorse and perhaps a touch of guilt. "I should have gone with her today," she murmured as she placed him on her shoulder. "Surely ignorant help is better than no help at all."

"But if you'd been with Kate, you couldn't have gone with Mr. Wilson," Mary said from her seat on the sofa, giving her sister a knowing smirk. "It would have been a shame to miss a drive in the park with a gentleman so clearly smitten with you."

"He's not smitten," Hannah argued feebly.

"He's not?" Mary's smirk grew. "Because I saw you arrive home. He lifted you down from the carriage without putting out the step, and he kissed your hand." She leaned in to add, "And don't pretend you didn't look back over your shoulder to watch him drive away."

Color climbed up Hannah's neck and into her cheeks. Nathaniel could feel the heat of her embarrassment glowing off of her. "That's enough, Mary. You're making much ado about nothing."

But it didn't feel like nothing to Nathaniel. Thinking of Wilson's hands on Hannah's waist to lift her from the curricle made him wish he were human so he could plant the man a facer. But the impulse fizzled at the thought of her turning to look back. A last look like that didn't speak of indifference.

Nathaniel was more convinced than ever not to tell Hannah about the Duchess of Harborough's suggestion. If she liked Wilson, he would not stand in her way, no matter the cost to himself. All that mattered was Hannah's happiness.

Chapter 15

"Did you find *anything* today?" Hannah asked Kate when they were seated in the library that night with Henry. "I'm so sorry I wasn't there—I'll go with you tomorrow and however many days we're still here. I shouldn't have put this all on you."

"It's my privilege," Kate said. "It's nice having a magical challenge to keep me occupied and distract me from how overwhelming I find Society." She smiled wryly. "I did try one spell this afternoon—obviously without success—and something else happened too." She described her meeting with the Duke of Harborough and his wife, and the duchess's suggestion. "Tempo may not be happy with me for mentioning it, he said it was too much to ask of you, but I think you have the right to know, since it's at least as much your choice as his."

Hannah stared at Kate for a long moment. "A kiss and a promise of marriage, and he'll be human again?" she repeated finally, convinced she'd misheard.

Kate nodded.

"It *is* a lot to ask," Henry grumbled. "Agreeing to marry a complete stranger with no idea of his character or his prospects…"

"She knows something of his character." Kate laid a gentle

hand over her husband's. "He defended her from Lord Trellion, and he wouldn't stand for Miss Chamberlain's unkindness. Even his refusal to demand this of her shows that he's a man of honor."

Hannah silently added that Tempo was patient, considerate, and a good listener. His compliments rang with honesty and kindness, not flattery. She'd grown quite fond of him. She could have declared that she knew enough to proceed without fear, except for one thing: her heart belonged to Johnson.

"I'll have to think on it," she said, forestalling any further argument from her brother, and changed to their other primary subject. "Have you had any news at all of Johnson?"

"None," Henry frowned. "No one has seen hide nor hair of him for weeks. Wortle was the last—they went out drinking a few nights before Mary's ball…." He trailed off, and his eyes grew wide. He looked from Hannah to Kate and back. "You don't think… Johnson is Tempo?"

Kate squeaked and pressed her hand to her mouth.

Hannah's jaw dropped. "He couldn't possibly—"

"It fits, though, doesn't it?" Henry said. "He vanished around the same time Tempo appeared. He'd been drinking, though Wortle had been so foxed he couldn't guess at how much Johnson had imbibed."

"But why wouldn't he tell me?" Hannah felt like she'd been kicked in the gut by a horse.

"He probably couldn't," Kate said. "Magic is like that sometimes."

"Or he may be embarrassed," Henry said, frowning. "He's small and weak, which isn't how he would want you, or any of us, to see him."

Hannah reluctantly admitted that they were both right. Her

mind raced, trying this hypothesis against what she knew of Tempo. Johnson would absolutely have come to her aid against Trellion. The compliments could have come from him too. Johnson was more of a talker than Tempo, though the difficulty of speaking could account for that, but both were exceptional listeners.

She excused herself. Sometimes talking through a problem helped, but sometimes it didn't, and though both Henry and Kate had some idea of how she felt for Johnson, she wanted to keep her pondering to herself.

Once in her nightclothes, she settled into bed with her book of wildflowers. Tempo hopped over to join her. She studied him out of the corner of her eye, wondering what he'd say if she asked him outright if he was Johnson. But she didn't want to put him on the spot. As Henry had pointed out, his condition was mortifying, as was how he came to be that way, and it would be unkind to poke at the sore place. And for all she knew, Henry's guess could be wrong and Tempo was someone else entirely.

But could two people really have disappeared so completely at the same time?

"Lady?" Tempo croaked. "Thinking?"

Hannah realized that she hadn't turned the page. "Yes, I'm afraid I'm thinking entirely too much to concentrate tonight."

The little frog stared at her patiently, waiting for her to elaborate. But tonight she wouldn't share.

"Several conversations today have given me food for thought, that's all." She closed the book and set it aside. She glanced at Tempo again before blowing out the candle and was surprised to see he looked sad. "Is something wrong, Tempo?"

"Nothing," he said. "Sweet. Dreams."

CHAPTER 15

Hannah had the distinct impression as he hopped back to his pillow that she wasn't the only one with complicated, secret thoughts.

She lay awake in the dark, allowing her mind to come at the problem from every direction. She remembered the night of her birthday, how upset she'd been that Johnson had apparently forgotten, and how defensive Tempo had seemed as he said *didn't forget*. She'd thought that he was comparing himself to Johnson, pointing out that *he'd* remembered what Johnson had missed. But had Johnson remembered, and she'd misunderstood?

The more she thought about it, the more convinced she was that poor Johnson was the frog sitting in the dark on the opposite side of her room. In which case, promising to marry him would set her up for happiness all her life, provided the duchess's suggestion worked. But what if he wasn't? What if Tempo regained his human form only to be a gentleman she'd never met before? She'd be bound to him for life, regardless of her feelings for the still-missing Nathaniel Johnson. She had no doubt that Tempo would treat her well. They could probably even be happy together. But was it worth the risk?

What other choice did she have? If she didn't kiss Tempo, she risked never seeing Johnson again. He'd be stuck as a frog for the rest of his short, miserable life, and her dream of marrying him would be dashed for good. She'd never know what they could have had together.

But what if he *was* Johnson and he didn't want her? What if she really was no more than a sister figure, a tagalong kid who was fun to tease and flirt with but could never be seen as more? What if his heart belonged to someone else? Had Kate been wrong about his reasons for not telling Hannah about this potential solution? Did he simply not want to marry her?

The sky was already fading to gray before Hannah finally began to doze. The last memory to play through her mind was of Tempo's contentment on her lap at the concert until Mr. Wilson joined them, and Mr. Wilson's conviction that Tempo didn't like him. Hannah had been unconvinced, but now a stray thought wondered if Tempo was jealous. Before Hannah could follow this thought further, she fell asleep.

***

The sun was climbing above the rooftops when Hannah woke. Normally she'd have been up by now, taking Tempo outside to eat his breakfast before she dressed and went downstairs for hers. But normally she would have gotten more than three or four hours of sleep. She sat up and stretched, her gaze automatically falling on the small frog. He was already asleep for the day, his sides gently moving as he breathed. The questions that had kept her up so late fell away into a kind of clarity: she simply had to know. She couldn't go the rest of her life wondering what if. If there was any chance at all that Tempo was Johnson, she had to try, even if it meant binding herself to someone else, even if Johnson would never be more than a friend and brother figure.

If nothing else, she owed Tempo, who'd proven himself a loyal friend time and again, to do what she could to save him.

She stood and crossed to the table with the little pillow, then paused. There was a good chance that nothing would come of this attempt. But if it *did* work, and if a gentleman *did* materialize in her bedchamber, it would be better if she was in something more than her nightclothes. She hurried into the next room and threw on a morning dress, suddenly impatient to have her questions answered, whether good or bad. She left her hair in its braid from the night, though she'd tossed and turned so much that it was half tumbled down. Returning to the bedroom, she crossed again to where Tempo snoozed on his embroidered pillow, oblivious.

Hannah leaned over and whispered, "I promise to marry you once you're human again." Then she bent a little farther and brushed her lips lightly over the smooth olive skin on Tempo's head.

An explosion sent Hannah stumbling back. The table fell over, shattering the basin and pitcher against the floor and splashing water over her bare feet. Her ears rang and spots glittered before her eyes, but the burst didn't seem to be made of sound or light or even air. It could only be magic. A tall, disheveled figure lay in a heap over the chair nearest the toppled table. She watched, shaken and breathless, as he straightened and pulled himself up to sit in the chair. His brown eyes were dazed and disoriented, and his sandy hair was a touch too long and beyond tousled. His clothing was rumpled, damp, and dirty.

But he was human.

Johnson's eyes, startled and confused, locked onto Hannah's. Shock and relief rushed through her, and her head spun. Her knees felt like jelly. She reached for the wall, the fallen table, the arm of the chair, anything to keep herself from collapsing. Johnson's hand found hers and tugged her to him, and she tumbled onto his lap.

"Why didn't you *tell* me?" she demanded in a whisper, banging her fist against his chest for emphasis as her eyes burned. "You *knew* how worried I was."

She tried to choke back the tears, but it was no use. She buried her face in his rumpled shoulder and sobbed. Johnson folded her into his arms, stroking her hair and whispering, "I'm sorry. I couldn't—I *tried*. Hannah, love, I'm so, *so* sorry."

The door to the dressing room crashed open. Kate called, "Hannah, what just *happened*? I felt magic—" She skidded to a halt in the bedroom doorway, Henry only a step behind her.

Hannah raised her head with a sniffle and a hiccup. Kate's curling golden hair hung loose around her shoulders, and she still held her hairbrush in one hand. Henry's cravat dangled around his neck as if he'd only just begun to tie it. Both of them gaped with mouths hanging open.

Hannah realized abruptly that she was sitting on a gentleman's lap. In her bedchamber. At least she'd gotten dressed first. "It worked," she said, her voice coming out about an octave higher than normal and squeaky. "I nearly fainted from shock. Johnson caught me before I fell."

Henry's mouth moved but nothing came out. Kate took a step nearer. Hannah kept her eyes on her sister-in-law because she seemed the most likely to recover her senses first. Kate dealt with magic regularly, after all.

But Kate was also expecting, and the shock and exertion at this time of morning had cleared the color from her face.

"Kate, why don't you and I both lie down for a bit." Hannah gestured to the bed. "Henry can ring the bell for breakfast to be brought up."

Her brother shook himself and pulled the bell cord. He helped Kate to Hannah's bed, where she sank down onto the edge, then lifted Hannah to her feet and helped her to sit beside his wife. Henry stood for a moment, looking between the two women and his friend in the chair.

CHAPTER 15

"I suppose that's our cue to leave," he said to Johnson. He offered a hand and pulled his friend to his feet, putting an arm around his shoulders and steering him out of the room.

Hannah watched them go before flopping backward, swiping the tears from her cheeks. Kate fell back beside her, staring silently at the ceiling for a moment. Then she giggled. The sound triggered something in Hannah. All the emotions of the past twelve hours came bubbling up as laughter, and the two of them lay helplessly, laughing until tears streamed from Hannah's eyes again and her sides hurt.

Chapter 16

Henry looked both ways before guiding Nathaniel into the hallway. A few yards along the empty passage, they ducked into another open doorway. Nathaniel stood just inside Henry's dressing room as his friend shoved the door closed behind them. Bottles of perfume on the vanity and a bonnet hanging off the back of a chair suggested that Henry shared this room with his wife. Nathaniel watched, still dazed and befuddled from the combination of magic and less than an hour of sleep, as his friend dug through his wardrobe, muttering.

Henry emerged with a crisp white shirt, a navy blue coat, and a starched cravat. "I'm afraid you're stuck with your own trousers and boots for now, but we can make the top half of you presentable."

Nathaniel shook himself from his stupor to strip off his clothes and replace them with the ones Henry held out. The sleeves were an inch or two short, but that was nothing to complain about. Henry offered him a comb for his hair, and he cringed when he saw his reflection in the mirror. Not how he wanted Hannah to see him, looking windblown and unkempt and in desperate need of a haircut.

A knock sounded at the door, and Henry went to retrieve the

breakfast tray that he'd presumably ordered for himself and Kate before the chaos in Hannah's room. He set it on a small table, then pulled up two chairs beside it. He sat in one and looked Nathaniel over as he came to take the other.

He nodded. "You look about how one would expect for traveling post through the night and arriving by hack early this morning."

Nathaniel blinked at him, one hand pausing midway through reaching for a scone. "Traveling post…?"

"Yes, of course," Henry said, pouring two cups of tea and pushing one toward Nathaniel. "You were called away on sudden, urgent business several weeks ago and have just now returned."

Nathaniel took a sip of the scorching tea, allowing his mind to catch up. "Right. Of course. Business so unexpected and consuming that I forgot to tell anyone where I was going."

"Precisely." Henry piled clotted cream and jam onto a scone and ate it in two bites. Nathaniel did the same, and the two ate silently for a few minutes until the tray was bare. Henry surveyed the empty tray and grinned. "Shall I call for more?"

"No," Nathaniel shook his head and raised his nearly empty cup. "Thank you. I shouldn't overdo it. I've subsisted on nothing but insects for weeks."

Henry grimaced, and Nathaniel laughed. His heart suddenly felt much lighter. "I'm sorry I couldn't tell you," he added, his smile fading. "I know how worried you all were."

"You can probably *guess*," Henry said pointedly, "but you were miles too far away to know for sure."

Nathaniel nodded slowly. "I *was* miles away. But your family is practically my family, and it was wrong of me to disappear without thinking how it would affect you."

"I'm willing to forgive and forget. You've been punished enough, I think." Henry grinned again, adding, "And you'll be punished more when Mother gets hold of you. A mother's ability to bestow guilt is legendary, and ours is one of the best."

Nathaniel chuckled. Continuing to build his false history, he said, "I did come back as soon as I could, once I realized my mistake."

Henry nodded. "Good man." He leaned forward and dropped his voice, fixing Nathaniel with a hard stare. "No one else need ever know. Hannah had nothing to do with this."

Nathaniel's wits had recovered enough over the course of breakfast to recognize the seriousness of the situation. He'd spent weeks in a far too intimate setting with Henry's sister, though he *had* been a frog, and he'd reappeared in her bedchamber and been found embracing her on his lap. His heart flopped like a caught fish, and he ran his hand over his face. Hannah's reputation was to be guarded at all costs, hence the importance of the lie. But holding her had felt so good...

"Well..." he said slowly, holding Henry's gaze, even as his friend's brows rose in challenge. "She *may* have had something to do with why I hurried back so quickly."

Henry's glare turned to a look of understanding. Nathaniel had never outright admitted to his friend how he felt about Hannah, but Henry knew him too well not to guess. Henry's mouth quirked up again at the corner. "She *was* dreadfully worried. I'm glad you don't take her feelings lightly."

"Never."

Henry rose and went to order the coach to take Nathaniel back to his own lodgings. He could only imagine the mess his affairs were in, having disappeared so suddenly and completely. But all he could think of right now was a bath and bed.

CHAPTER 16

Before long, Nathaniel was climbing into the carriage and saying goodbye to Henry.

"Come to dinner tonight," Henry said, shaking his hand. "Mother has been beside herself, and you might as well get the guilt over with."

Nathaniel accepted the invitation, less for Henry's family than from a need to talk to Hannah. He wished he could have talked to her before he left this morning. He suspected he knew what she'd done to remove the spell, but he needed to hear it from her. And what about Wilson? Was the conversation she'd shared with him on their drive one that had supplied food for distracted thought last night?

Now that he was human again, Nathaniel wouldn't give up to his rival without a fight. He wanted above all for Hannah to be happy, but he desperately needed to convince her that *he* was the one to make her happy, not Wilson.

***

Two hours later, Nathaniel woke, disoriented, in his own bed. He'd found his valet in the perfectly arranged dressing room, reading a book as if Nathaniel had only slept later than usual and not been absent for a month. Smithers had seemingly accepted the story of his master's urgent business without question, though Nathaniel thought the man was offended at having been left behind. Nathaniel had removed coat, cravat, and boots and fallen into bed. Now he frowned up at Smithers, who stood over him.

"You asked that I not let you sleep past two hours, sir," the valet said. "A bath is waiting in the other room for you."

"Thank you." Nathaniel rubbed his face. His jaw was rough

with stubble, and his mouth felt dry and sticky.

It took more than an hour for Smithers to bring him back to his usual smart appearance, including a shave and a trim. Once he felt more like the man he ought to be, Nathaniel ordered his horse and went out. He had an errand with a jeweler on Bond Street before he returned to Berkeley Square. Perhaps if he stopped at a florist as well, he could avoid some of the punishing guilt coming his way.

***

Nathaniel entered the Duke of Caulder's drawing room an hour before dinner would usually be served, carrying an enormous bouquet of tulips. The flowers were a veritable rainbow, imported from Holland. The duchess and Mary gasped when he was announced, getting up and rushing to greet him. Henry and Kate, who'd been sitting with them, followed more slowly behind, smiling.

"Nathaniel, my dear boy, *where* have you *been?*" Her Grace grasped one of his hands in both of hers. "We've been worried *sick* about you, haven't we, Henry? I would swear we've asked half the residents of London if they've seen or heard from you."

"I am most heartily sorry." Nathaniel bent to brush a kiss over her cheek. "You've been as dear to me as my own mother, and I would never wish to cause you a moment's unhappiness. I had unexpected, urgent business that called me out of town. I confess, I was so caught up in it that it didn't occur to me to tell anyone until much later."

"Are these apology tulips, then?" Mary asked. "I forgive you already."

Nathaniel laughed and let her take the bouquet from him.

She arranged them in the large vase that a servant immediately presented. "Thank you, Lady Mary. Will you forgive me as well, Your Grace?"

She smiled and squeezed his hand. "I suppose I must. I'm too happy to see you here and well to hold a grudge. But I shan't forgive you next time," she said with mock sternness. "Henry did tell us that you stopped by early this morning to assure us you were all right."

"Yes, I came as soon as I arrived by post." Nathaniel caught Henry's eye and grinned. "He thought I wasn't presentable enough to see you then—I was decidedly battered and travel worn, nothing like the dashing lordling you're used to seeing."

Henry's mother continued to fuss over him for a few more minutes, before Nathaniel asked, "Where is Lady Hannah? I need to apologize to her as well, and for missing her birthday."

"I think she's reading in the breakfast room," Mary said. "Shall I go fetch her?"

"I'll go myself, if I may."

Excused, Nathaniel crossed to the breakfast room and pushed open the door. Hannah was sitting at the table with a book in front of her, but he'd spent enough time with her lately to know that she wasn't reading. He wondered how long the book had been open to that page. She looked up when he entered, and the way her eyes lit up when she saw him, the smile that brightened her face to rival the sun's brilliance, stunned him. She jumped to her feet and rushed to take his hands. Her hands felt small and soft in his, and she was shorter than he remembered: petite, dainty, and perfectly lovely. Everything he'd thought to say fled his mind as he stared into her sparkling hazel eyes.

Chapter 17

Hannah tried to ignore the fizz of lightning up her arms from where her hands clasped Johnson's, tried to pretend she wasn't smiling like a loon. But the way he was looking at her…. She took a shaky breath.

"We—we should probably talk about what happened this morning," she said softly.

He nodded slowly. "We should." He seemed to gather his thoughts. "What did you do?"

"Kate told me that if I agreed to marry you—" His expression went blank, sort of hollow, and her heart sank. "Is something wrong?" Her fear from the night before that he'd rather have a different wife returned. "Why didn't you want me to?" she whispered.

"I didn't want to put you under an obligation," he rasped, his voice rougher than she'd ever heard it. "I didn't want to take advantage of your kind heart. You deserve better."

Hannah swallowed back the fear that choked her. She'd chosen this path, and now she would walk it. "And if I'm happy with my choice?" she breathed.

"Are you?" His eyes widened. "And not only because you were worried about me?"

"Yes, you goose." She shook her head, exasperated. "I was

worried about you because I've been sweet on you forever. Why else would I follow the three of you around so much when you stayed with us? Ask Henry—I didn't bother my brothers nearly as often when you weren't there."

Johnson's mouth worked, but nothing came out. She could practically see him rearranging the pieces of reality as he knew it to make a new picture. "But what about Wilson?" he asked finally, a shadow darkening his rich brown eyes. "He's made no secret of his intentions."

"And I've made it clear that he is a friend and will never be more. My heart is already spoken for."

A flame lit behind Johnson's eyes. He took a step closer, letting go of one of her hands to raise his own. He slid his fingers into her hair, his palm cradling her neck, his thumb stroking her cheek. Hannah's breath caught, and her heart tripped over itself as it raced. He bent toward her, slowly, tentatively. Hannah tipped her head up, her eyelids fluttering closed as he pressed his lips against hers. Hannah felt like another magic explosion was going off inside of her. Her arms slipped up around his neck of their own accord, and his free arm came around her waist and pulled her closer. Kissing Johnson was better than she'd ever imagined, sweet and spicy, heartrending and breathtaking and miraculous.

A throat clearing from the doorway startled them apart, but neither let go enough to pull back more than a few inches. Both of their heads turned to see Henry standing just inside the door, brows raised and arms crossed.

Hannah felt a surge of annoyance toward her favorite brother. "He's proposing," she hissed. "Go *away*."

Henry grinned. "You have exactly five minutes." He disappeared through the door and closed it firmly behind him.

Johnson turned back to Hannah and rested his forehead against hers. "Have I not done that yet?" She shook her head the tiniest bit side to side. "I didn't plan a speech for this. My goal for today was simply to convince you not to marry Wilson."

He tipped his head and stole another quick kiss. Hannah smiled and bit her lower lip. "Consider me thoroughly convinced."

Johnson grinned. He let his arms settle around her waist, holding her loosely so that he could back up enough to look into her eyes. "I love you, Hannah. You're everything I've always wanted. I need you in my life." He winked and added, "Especially now that I know how intoxicating it is to be close to you."

It struck Hannah suddenly that Johnson had spent weeks riding around in her pocket or on her shoulder, and she remembered how his eyes had closed in bliss as she stroked along his head and back. Warmth thrilled through her, and she shivered.

Misinterpreting the shiver, Johnson pulled her closer again, wrapping his arms around her and bending to whisper in her ear, "Marry me, Lady?"

Tempo's name for her triggered another shiver. How did he manage to make a title sound so sweet and seductive and endearing all at the same time?

"I will," she whispered back.

By the time Henry returned a minute later—this time knocking before pushing the door open—they'd finished kissing and were holding hands. They were, perhaps, standing a bit closer together than was quite proper, but Hannah couldn't bring herself to step back.

Dinner was a happier meal than they'd had since Johnson's

disappearance, and he insisted on Mary telling him all about what he'd missed of her first Season. He apologized profusely for missing her coming-out ball, and listened attentively to the rest, only darting glances at Hannah every so often. Hannah fought to keep her smile under control. She was just so *happy*, and each time Mary detailed an event that Johnson had in fact secretly attended, she bit her lips to smother the smirk. Johnson's glances at those moments didn't help, because his eyes sparkled with humor and secrets.

They'd agreed that he would talk to her father after the ladies adjourned to the drawing room. Hannah was of age, so she didn't officially need Father's permission to wed, but this was worth doing right.

Hannah was barely across the threshold of the drawing room before she spilled the news to Mama, Mary, and Kate.

"I can't contain it a moment longer," she blurted. "Johnson asked me to marry him!"

The gasps and delighted squeals were exactly what Hannah expected.

"You said yes, of course." Mary ran across the room. "You've been violently in love with him forever."

"I wouldn't say 'violently,'" Hannah mumbled into her sister's smothering hug.

"Naturally, she said yes." Mama shooed Mary aside so that she could embrace Hannah herself. "He's an excellent match and a good man, and she gets dreamy whenever he's near. She has all her life."

Hannah's mouth fell open. "Have I been that obvious?"

"Yes," all three women said together.

The gentlemen didn't wait long before joining them. Hannah's father immediately gave her a hug, tears glistening in the corners of his eyes. She beamed and kissed his cheek.

"You'll be happy," he said gruffly.

"I'm already the happiest girl in the world, Father."

He nodded and went to join Mama on the couch. Johnson came to stand beside Hannah, resting one hand on her lower back. He murmured in her ear, "You ought to have a ring. I'm sorry I wasn't prepared."

Hannah smiled up at him. "You exceeded your goal for today. I'm content with promises." And kisses, though Hannah wasn't sure she could ever have enough of those to be content.

"You'll have one soon. I already ordered it."

"Even though you thought I liked Mr. Wilson?"

Johnson shrugged, and his mouth quirked up at the corner. "I did think it would take longer to convince you that you couldn't live without me, but I was determined to succeed." He leaned in even closer so that his breath tickled her ear. "Because *I* can't live without *you*."

Warmth spread all through Hannah, and she was so glad she'd taken the risk this morning of kissing the frog.

***

Johnson had always been a welcome figure at their house, but now he was a daily visitor. The morning after the proposal, he arrived with two horses and invited Hannah to go riding.

"You missed riding," she said with a smile as he helped her into the saddle.

"I missed riding *with you*," he corrected. "All the things I missed most involved you in some way."

"Boxing? Cards?"

"I didn't miss boxing most," he shrugged. "And you found a

way to improve greatly on the game of whist."

Hannah laughed, blushing at the memory of how Tempo had leaned into her neck. She was still getting used to the idea that he'd been Johnson all along.

They rode toward the park at a leisurely pace. "Will you have tea with us after?" Hannah asked. "Mama will want to talk wedding plans."

"Surely that's more your domain than mine."

"Perhaps. But I expect you'll want a say in some things. Like how soon the wedding will be held."

"Tomorrow," he said quickly. "I'll get a special license." He met Hannah's grin with one of his own. "I'm teasing, but it shouldn't be too long. What if someone finds out where I've been all this time?"

The scandal that would follow such a discovery would be outrageous.

"Will you invite your father?"

Johnson's smile promptly fell. "What good would that do?"

Hannah guided her borrowed mare closer to his side so that she could reach out and squeeze his hand. "I know he's been an awful father, Johnson, but I don't want you to have the same regrets Kate has. You can't force him to come, but you can make an effort to include him."

He frowned at his horse's mane for a long moment. "I'll invite him on one condition."

"What is it?"

"You call me Nathaniel." His brown eyes found and held hers. "Johnson's what my friends call me, but you're so much more than a friend."

Butterflies filled Hannah. She bit her lips and nodded. Johnson's smile returned as brightly as ever.

After a long, peaceful ride, they returned to the house, where, as expected, Mama awaited them. After some debate, they set a date for three weeks out. Mama agreed with Kate and Henry that they could delay their return to Cauldercrest a while longer. Johnson—Nathaniel—agreed to write his father express so that if Lord Bembry did choose to come, he'd have time to travel from Devon. If he didn't, well, they'd be going out to Devon in a few weeks for Johnson's annual visit anyway.

Hannah's next week was filled with visits to the modiste for wedding clothes and other necessary arrangements. After the third morning with Madame Evangeline, during which Mama insisted on yet another new gown, Hannah excused herself for the afternoon to finally paint watercolors with Kate. Johnson came to dinner that evening, and he grinned unsympathetically when Hannah complained about her morning, saying that he had filled the time with an invigorating bout with Gentleman Jackson. Hannah scowled at him, but her ire was short-lived—she'd missed his smile and his laugh and his sparkling eyes too much to hold a grudge.

On Wednesday evening, they all went to Almack's. Johnson was swarmed by acquaintances curious to know where he'd been for so long. He pawned them off with the story of urgent business in the country, then made a quick escape to dance the first set with Hannah.

"You have no idea what torture it was to watch you dance with everyone but me," he told her as they took their places.

Hannah couldn't remember ever enjoying an Almack's assembly so much, and she was disappointed when the music stopped. Johnson leaned close and murmured, "Save me the waltz," before turning to Mary. "I never apologized properly for standing you up at your coming-out ball. May I make up

CHAPTER 17

for it now?"

He led her to the floor, and Hannah smiled to watch them. She danced a set with Lord Marcell, then Mr. Wilson asked for the next. As they took their places in the set, he gave her dress a once over. Noting the lack of sash, he said, "No Tempo tonight?"

Hannah shook her head. "I released him." It was the truth, if not in the way he thought. "As much as I liked having him with me, he deserved his freedom."

He nodded solemnly. "Ah. Very kind of you. It's probably in the best interest of the local fauna, stopping the trend of tiny pets before it really begins."

Hannah laughed. "I'm not sure frogs ever stood much chance of becoming a trend. I expect I'll always be an outlier."

"An original," Mr. Wilson corrected gallantly.

When the song ended, he escorted her off the floor. Johnson met them there as the first strains of a waltz began. The two gentlemen eyed each other, and Hannah was suddenly uncomfortable. She laid a hand on Johnson's arm. "Have you two met?"

Mr. Wilson nodded. "Johnson. Good to see you back."

Johnson covered Hannah's hand with his free one. "Thank you, Wilson. If you'll excuse us?"

Mr. Wilson's gaze landed on their joined hands, and his eyes found Hannah's. She saw understanding dawn, and he made her a small bow before turning back to Johnson. He held out a hand. "You're a lucky man."

Johnson shook it. "The luckiest."

Hannah breathed a sigh of relief as Mr. Wilson walked away. "How awkward," she muttered.

"I might as well admit how unbearably jealous I was every

time he was near you," Johnson said. "I really did glower at him all through that concert."

Hannah laughed. Johnson slipped one hand around her back and took her free hand in his. The warmth and strength of his hands, his closeness, the scent of his cologne—it all combined to leave Hannah giddy and breathless as they joined the twirling couples.

The final bars of the song brought Hannah back to earth. They stopped moving, but Johnson made no move to release her. He looked down at her, his eyes full and intense. She beamed up at him.

"Did you notice, Nathaniel, that you haven't once stepped on my toes tonight?"

"It's because I'm walking on air with you," he murmured. "My feet haven't touched the floor all evening."

***

A week later, Johnson joined them early for breakfast. He leaned to whisper to Hannah as he went to his seat at the table. "Will you walk with me?"

She nodded, and as soon as the meal was over, they slipped out of the house. Johnson—he'd always be Johnson, the boy she'd fallen in love with, even now that she could call him Nathaniel—brought her to the back garden. She noticed that he gave the rubbish heap and its attendant flies a wide berth as they made their way to a secluded bench beneath a shade tree.

They settled on the bench, and Johnson took her hand in his, turning it over and tracing his finger over her palm. "I received a letter from my father this morning."

His expression was unreadable, his voice flat, and that told

CHAPTER 17

Hannah all she needed to know. Still, she asked, "What did he say?"

"He offered his congratulations, but he won't be attending the wedding."

Sighing, Hannah brushed her fingers over his cheek. "His choices are his to make," she murmured, echoing sentiments she'd said to Kate. "But I'm proud of you for asking."

He caught her fingers and kissed their tips, then held both of her hands in his. "He still expects us to visit in Devon after we're married."

Hannah could tell it bothered him that his father wouldn't come for his only son's wedding yet had the effrontery to insist they delay their honeymoon to cater to his schedule. "The estate is near the shore, is it not?" She said gently. "Spending part of the summer by the seaside wouldn't be such a terrible thing."

Johnson's expression lightened somewhat. "You always see the good," he said, leaning in to kiss her cheek. "I love that about you." They settled more comfortably against the back of the bench, and Hannah rested her head against his shoulder as his arm came around her. This was a perfect moment, and soon such moments wouldn't have to be snuck in a private corner of her parents' garden.

"I've taken a house for us," Johnson said after a long, peaceful silence. "Just outside of town. The drive to assemblies and dinner parties will be longer, but we'll have our own space, and we won't have to escape to the country for the summer once the heat and smell of London becomes unbearable. We can take our time and decide when and where to go, if we want to leave at all." He kissed the top of her head. "It's a sweet house with a big garden. I think you'll like it."

"I'll like anywhere if we're together." Hannah's eyes drifted closed as she snuggled closer.

"There's one more thing." Johnson fidgeted with his pocket for a second and sat up straighter, so Hannah opened her eyes and straightened too. When he turned to her, he held a golden ring in his hand. The band was plain, but centered in the top was a golden flower with five rounded petals cupping a glittering diamond.

Hannah's mouth fell open. "It's a—"

A buttercup.

"I didn't forget your birthday." Johnson's mouth quirked up as he took her hand and slipped the ring onto her finger. "As it happens, when a frog gives you a buttercup, it means 'I adore you.'"

Hannah couldn't tear her eyes from the ring. "Does it indeed?"

"It's what *I* meant," he said, kissing her temple, her cheek, her jaw. She turned her face to meet his, and his lips found hers in an explosion of joy.

Epilogue

Fourteen Months Later

Nathaniel wearily opened the door from the library to the garden and took a deep breath. The crisp autumn air filled and refreshed him, bringing him back to full alertness. He'd missed that about the Bembry estate. His father's toxic presence had made him forget how much he loved the place.

But he was here now and here to stay. He'd spent the last three hours in the cellars with the butler, sorting through his father's wine collection and deciding what to keep and what to sell off. All the claret would go, and the few bottles of gin. Claret had been half the reason his father had been such a lackluster husband and parent, in addition to contributing to his early demise, and blue ruin had been the cause of Nathaniel's own—blessedly temporary—misfortune. He'd sworn it off his very first day as a frog and hadn't touched a drop since. The butler, Phillips, had poorly hidden his dismay at selling off what appeared to be half the contents of the cellars, but Nathaniel was adamant. His father's vices had no place in this house any longer.

Now he stepped farther into the garden, and his gaze fell on the reason he so firmly repudiated the previous earl's legacy. Hannah sat on a bench, her silky brown hair loosely braided and pinned so that wisps drifted around her face in the breeze. She wore no bonnet, and she tilted her head so that the sun fell warm across her cheeks. Her freckles would never fade at this rate, and he loved it. She balanced a book of blank pages on her rounded belly, sketching the arbor opposite her bench.

Nathaniel watched his beautiful wife, marveling again that she loved him and had even been willing to kiss a frog to be with him. Hannah was all sweetness and kindness and warmth, and she deserved everything good. For her, he would be the best husband he could be, the opposite of his father in every way, and he would be his best for their child as well.

Hannah glanced up and saw him, and she smiled and patted the bench beside her. Nathaniel joined her there, resting his arm around her shoulders on the bench behind her.

Her hazel eyes caressed his face. "You look exhausted."

He smiled wryly. "I didn't know putting my father's affairs in order would be so much work."

Hannah nodded sympathetically. "I expect it's always like that." She closed her sketchbook and set it aside. "Mama wrote that she and Papa and Henry are coming for the funeral. They're probably halfway here by now. Mary's staying with Kate and little Amelia, since it's still too soon for them to travel so far."

Nathaniel squeezed her shoulder. "Your family has been so good to me," he said.

He left it unspoken that her family had been better than his own, though he was sure Hannah heard it in his silence. His own mother had been loving and gracious, but she had been unhappy all her married life. He resented his father for that, for allowing her to be miserable all those years. He resented him, too, for not only unintentionally missing Nathaniel's adulthood, including the birth of his first child, but also for all the years he'd willfully missed out on while he was still alive.

EPILOGUE

The Earl of Bembry's death was a bitter thing, and Nathaniel couldn't predict at any moment whether he'd next be swamped by grief or rage.

Hannah rested a hand on his knee. "You're allowed to mourn him, Nat. For what he ought to have been as well as for what he was."

He laid his hand over hers, and she leaned her head against his shoulder. He kissed her temple. They sat silently like this for a long while, comfortably together, supporting each other.

Suddenly, Hannah gave a little, "oh!" of surprise, followed by a giggle. She lifted her head and looked at him, her eyes sparkling. She took his hand and moved it to the swell of her belly, holding it there for a moment until he felt it too—the tiniest thump of a foot against his palm. His eyes shot to hers, awestruck and amazed, only to lose himself in her bright, joyful gaze. When he'd dreamed of marrying Hannah, he'd never imagined such perfect moments. He'd never known his heart could soar so high or fill to bursting or sing with the angels as it seemed to be doing right now.

Nathaniel leaned forward and kissed his wife, hoping to show her some of how he felt. Another, much more emphatic kick from the baby a minute later broke them apart. Grinning, they cuddled back against the bench, Hannah's head again on his shoulder, their hands still intertwined over their little one.

"Have you told them?" he asked.

Hannah nodded, smiling down at their joined hands. "Mama's ecstatic, naturally. She said Papa cried when he heard, but I don't know if I believe it—I've only seen him with tears in his eyes once or twice."

"I believe it," Nathaniel said. "He has a soft heart, and you're his little girl."

"Just imagine the watering pot he'll be when Mary gets married and has children, then," Hannah laughed. "Kate might have been the most excited, though. She's overjoyed that Amelia will have cousins." She slanted a look up at him. "You do know how Kate feels about cousins, don't you?"

Nathaniel laughed. "I do, and I share her fascination. As an only child, siblings were a dream, and cousins seemed like something only found in storybooks."

Hannah laughed too. "Well, you both get to share all the Stanton siblings, and we have enough cousins to go round too. I *am* glad our children will have cousins, though. I love a full house at Christmas."

Nathaniel's heart warmed at the thought. "How many children are you expecting, my love?"

"Just the one at the moment," she said lightly. "But he or she won't be our last, Lord Bembry." He cringed at the title and her smile turned wry. "You'll have to get used to it eventually, Nat."

"But not from you, Lady Bembry." He kissed the tip of her nose. "It took long enough to break you of calling me Johnson." She tipped her head to receive a kiss on the lips, which he willingly gave. "I've known it was coming eventually, but it's uncomfortable when one's identity shifts."

"It is uncomfortable," she agreed. "But that's not always a bad thing."

"No." He pulled her closer and rested his cheek against her hair. He'd gone from bachelor to frog to fiancé to husband within the last year and a half, and he didn't regret a bit of it, because it all led to him being here with Hannah. Being the new Earl of Bembry came with all kinds of emotional baggage he'd have to sort through, but even this wasn't entirely bad. The estate in Devon was theirs now, and they could raise their

EPILOGUE

children in the country, surrounded by nature and wonder and love.

For the first time in the weeks since they'd come to Devon to attend his father in his final brief illness, Nathaniel felt something within himself settle. Here with Hannah, in the place that he loved, he was home.

***

Thank you for reading Hannah and Nathaniel's story! I hope you enjoyed it as much as I did. If you loved it, please leave a review on Goodreads or your favorite retailer to help another reader find a book they'll love.

It means so much to me that you've taken the time to experience my alternate Regency England. If you missed Kate and Henry's story, you can find it in Her Enchanted Tower. *And if you're curious about the Duke and Duchess of Harborough, their story is told in* The Beast's Magician.

If you want to learn more and be the first to know about upcoming books (including the next in the Regency Magic Faerie Tales, The Sea-Bear's Wife, *coming in 2025), cover reveals, freebies, and other goodies, join my newsletter at elizaprokopovits.com/newsletter.*

Happy reading!
Eliza

Also By Eliza Prokopovits

Ember and Twine

Jewels and Dragons

The Thunderstone Theft

Regency Magic Faerie Tales
   Her Fae Secret
   The Beast's Magician
   Her Forgotten Sea
   Her Cursed Apple
   Her Enchanted Tower
   Her Accidental Frog

About the Author

Eliza Prokopovits (pro-COP-o-vits) is a writer and knitting designer. She is obsessed with books, yarn, and dark chocolate. She lives in Pennsylvania with her husband, two boys, and aging goldendoodle. She can occasionally be found on Instagram and Facebook.

www.ingramcontent.com/pod-product-compliance
Ingram Content Group UK Ltd.
Pitfield, Milton Keynes, MK11 3LW, UK
UKHW022210230426

12048UKWH00016BA/753